THE ETERNAL BATTLES

FALLEN STARS

Kadesh Sanders

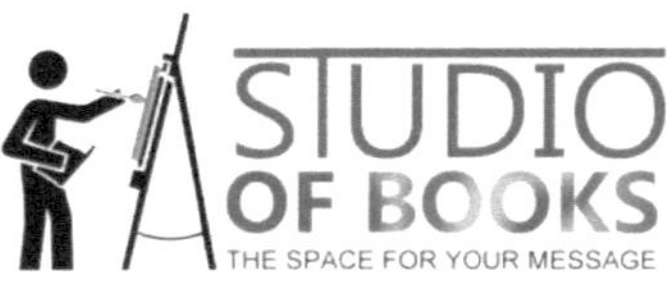

Studio of Books LLC
5900 Balcones Drive Suite 100
Austin, Texas 78731
www.studioofbooks.org
Hotline: (254) 800-1183

Ordering Information:
Special discounts are available on quantity purchases by corporations, associations, and others. For details, contact the publisher at the address above.

Printed in the United States of America.

ISBN-13:   Softcover   978-1-964864-89-1
           Hardcover   978-1-964864-90-7
           eBook   978-1-964864-91-4

Library of Congress Control Number: 2024925956

Table of Contents

CHAPTER 1

End of an era

And he opened the bottomless pit; and there arose a smoke out of the pit, as the smoke of a great furnace; and the sun and the air were darkened by reason of the smoke of the pit. - Revelation 9:2

"At that time Michael, the great prince who protects your people, will arise… - Daniel 12:1

SATAN IN THE ABYSS

The air was thick with black smoke in the abyss. Following the Lord's momentous arrival, Satan and his kingdom were imprisoned for centuries. Striking them down to the lowest depths of the pit. Satan and his demons are put to shame, locked in a network of brimstone-filled caverns deep in near the care of the earth. It wasn't as bad when the demons could come as they pleased. Their breathing labored because of volcanic ash inhalation. In the abyss, there was no light from the sun, just a reddish-orange hazy glow from the flames. No plants, just demonic monstrous creatures and worms, spiders, scorpions, and millipedes that never die. The only thing the evil entities could do while imprisoned by the Lord of Hosts was constantly thinking of the revenge they wanted to take against the Saints and holy angels. Their already living hatred of God and humans, made in His image as spirit beings clothed in flesh, was further cultivated and grew beyond any human comprehension. They are ready to pounce on the world. That's not the only thing on their mind. All of the evil continually flashes in their mind, drowning them in guilt suppressed by pride. Satan, Satana, the anti-Christ, Lilith, Jezebel, Bak'tor, Bezzulbub, Belial, Python, and Aberdeen were separated in different areas of the abyss as punishment for their war on creation. The souls of the coven and eclipse were repaid in full for their evil, joining in the punishment with the demons. God imprisoned Leviathan at the lowest depths of the sea and chained it with spiritual chains that tighten with movement. Near the abyss, there was a large window in the deep ocean cavern that allowed Leviathan to see inside. All of Hell screeched, roared, and snarled at God and against those who dwell in heaven. On Earth, humanity has had relative peace for the last 887 years. There were still some regional and civil wars and common criminality, but nothing like the demonic rebellion hundreds of years ago. Humanity flourished without demonic influence, and technology and knowledge advanced. Most people lived righteously and followed God, and others still worshipped demon Gods and practiced witchcraft. Others were in the valley of decision not following God or Satan but living by their own intellect or putting faith in the Earth and Universe. The Idolators rebuilt the coven at

Frost-peak in honor of the sorcerers who came before them and expanded the coven's reach into the forest at Duskmare Hollow. They were going to be under the radar so as not to alert anyone to their activities. The Church Had grown the most, with Billions Following Jesus Christ; They Expanded to multiple locations in the country of Avaloria, the capital city Avalon City, and the town of Willowbrook. The Church is led by a council of Prophets, Apostles, Pastors, Evangelists, and teachers, each serving a specific function in God's Ministry.The President of Avaloria, President Ethan Blackwell, and Vice President Garret Morgan led Avalaria, one of the largest countries on earth. Avaloria is a beautiful country with diverse biomes: Forest, tundra, desert, coastland, and mountains. The nation has the most animals and living nature on earth. The cities of Avalaria are large and robust, with tall skyscrapers and intricate highway systems, top-of-the-line bullet trains, and a metro. The streets are full of people, and new construction is occurring all across the nation. There are 70 provinces throughout Avalaria. The Economy is the first tier of capitalism that breeds innovation and competition. The nation of Avalaria has a Constitution and bill of rights like America, a free, mostly Christian country with a powerful military. Congress has two parties: one that believes in God, and the other that is a secular party. Avalaria's Sentinel Army Forces have a long reputation for being victorious warriors, protecting the people of Avalaria and the world from both people and Demons. There are many countries in the world; back when the Demon War happened, the Avalaria joined a world union and army of combined world powers to fight off the Eclipse army and the demons. There are 80 nations other than Avalaria. Most are friendly, but some Strongly dislike Avalrias devotion to The God of Creation, who Dwells Between the cherubims. President Ethan Blackwell and General Alexander Stormheart tasked the military and scientists to develop the space program and military training and preparedness as a tradition. people have long life spans in this world. Far away throughout the solar system and beyond planets full of demons and ruled by Mighty fallen angels. There two extra planets, Infernia, settled by demons, and Xenovia, where the fallen angels live. After the Fall of Samuel Lucifer now, Satan Rebelled in heaven and launched a war on earth. The Fallen Angels lay low and did not get involved with the first Demonic War because God would have Sealed them to like Satan's kingdom.So they stood down to bide their time. They built a galactic network across the galaxy with armies of demons and fallen angels to Fight God's forces. In Heaven, God's glory shines throughout the beautiful gardens and lush forests and mountains full of fruits and, flowers, trees; there were also animals of every kind, even some animals we don't yet know about. The Majestic nature is one million times the most beautiful site on our earth. On the edges of the golden cities. The Streets are of gold, door nobs made of pearl, and bricks made of diamonds in this realm, cities full of majestic royal mansions for the most faithful to god and righteousness. Everything from communal living to castles. Every precious stone and jewel is used in constructing every part of the heavenly cities:, Sapphire, Emerald, Topaz, Onyx, Beryl, Jade, Amethyst, Rubies, Diamond and gold, etc. The Ancient of days sees and knows all, so he tells Jesus Christ, his son and king of kings, The Commanders of The Heavenly Host of Angels. He who has all power in heaven, in the second heaven, on earth, and under the earth in the abyss. Jesus orders Micheal, The General of his Force of mighty angelic warriors, to prepare his troops for the next war with the Evil ones, as the seal will soon be released. Micheal responds, "Of course, My Lord, as You command, I arrange a meeting of the military counsel," and he swiftly flies giant orange flaming wings flapping like chariots, toward the military HQ of Heaven and " I Summon all Arch-Angels to discuss urgent matters from the ancient of days".Gabriel,Raphael,Uriel,Haniel,Castello,

Jophiel, Sophia, And Esther Zapped into the meet at the HQ in a second. Micheal announced, " Welcome, Brothers and Sisters, all The Hosts of Heaven's Armies. Another Angel, Ena Katsumi, attended the meeting. The Ancient of days has ordered us to prepare for war against the evil ones as they are about to be released"! The Angel stood firm, ready to fulfill The Lord's command, and Shouted in victory ready to begin training as soon as possible. Jophiel spoke," The Weapons of our warfare

are not carnal, but they are mighty through God to the pulling down of strongholds." (2 Corinthians 10:4), and she began to sing in power, activating her power of ice and fire. The Heavenly hosts Shouted Amen!! They prepared to go to the throne room of God to acknowledge the decree. Millions of warrior angels in power enter Before the lord God, The Holy Spirit, and Jesus glorious light shining on their faces. The angel began to worship the lord, saying Blessing and Honor, and glory forever be to our God"! Just as righteous are your Judgments and decrees, we will follow your voice. We accept your commandment, and we will prepare for war and fulfill our duty to defend your creation! The lord stood and blessed his soldiers and the fire of the holy spirit strengthened their heavenly powers. The Angels flew swiftly from the throne room to ready their armor and sharpen their weapons to begin training for the next battle. Micheal spoke, saying, "we'll need all hands on deck so everyone gets to take part!" The angels gathered in the different training areas and divisions, Dauling with their comrades to prepare for battle. Led by the Arch-Angel chiefs.

HEAVENLY CITY

The angels used Ancient weapons like swords, spears, Axes, Javilens, shields, guandaos, bow staffs, and Some Guns. One important thing should be known: not all angels have wings. Although most do, some angels look like regular humans, animal humanoids, beings of light fire. Some angels can even take the form of objects. They can teleport locations and transition between realms according to the assignment God needs the angel to fulfill. Angels have seven classifications. The first class is Seraphim, six-winged fiery angels. Two wings cover their face, two wings cover their feet, and with two wings, they fly. Their appearance is like burning coals in a fire and glorious faces of light. Seraphim fly closest to God's throne, worshiping God with power and burning love for the creator of all things. Seraphim are also called (The Burning Ones). The Cherabim angels are the second class of the angelic order. They have the likeness of a man and have four faces: that of a man, a lion (on the right side), and ox (on the left side), and an eagle, eyes all over. Cherbims are also close to Gods throne worshiping him. The third class of angels are called Ophanim were described be ezekiel as Golden wheels within wheels of enormous and dreadful size with eyes all over. They are see as heavenly charort or thrones of judgement for God. These three are of the highest order of angels. In Second Order of angels Dominions are the angels that God created to ensure the divine laws of God kingdom and creations are in perfect alignment and they rule over most angels and the universe. Virtues are angels in charge of all the elements God created and they also deliver miracles to people who prayed for them. They take a human for of light on earth appearing to strengthen and encourage faith in God. The Powers Angels are Gods Authorites they have power of the evil to limit its affect and restrain satans attacks on the world. Powers also are in charge of who get to rule a country and if the are following Gods laws andd need to be judged.Principality Angels are governing angels who preside over nation, groups of people, regions,and institutions, and they have a band of angels under their command about 300-600 angels. The Arch-angels are The Armed forces of God they go out and Fight For Heaven and God's people. They are the second to lowest rank in the angelic order. They appear and armored people with flaming wings or beings of light with enormous power to fight Demons ad fallen angels. Each Arch-angel commander presides over thousands of regular soldier angels.

The last class of Angels are Regular angels they appear to look like people with or without wings. They help,support, teach and protect individuals, Guardian angels are among this class seen as beings of light with swords guard those who belong to God. Micheal Clade in his golden armor with his orange flaming sword and blazing flaming wings with bronze skin. Begins to Spare with Gabriel Clade in Gold and blue-white armor blazing with blue flames, wielding his fiery sword and halberd. The two Arch-angels chiefs clash with tremendous power, sharpening their skills with each blow. Michael "It's been a a while since we've had to fight". Gabriel responded, " Yeah Mike it's great to dust off the weapons and Crush evil"! Mike" Oh yeah are you really ready?, Haaah Slash. Gabe "Of course I'm ready that was nothing let me show you how it's done, CLiiiing classh. Mike and Gabe use their fire powers orange and blue flames flicker all around as the two generals go head to head.

Next up Ralphel a Arch- Angel with gold and green armor wielding a fiery green Indian spear. His flames wicked about as he swung his spear. Raphael is powerful yet very humble. He has the ability to heal allies and people. Uriel clade in yellow and golden armor wielding a yellow spear flashing with lighting and yellow flames uriel has a lot of wisdom conserving the universe. He can control holy lighting from heaven. Ralph and Uri clash into a sparing match. Green flames and yellow lightning swirl around ralph "I see you've gotten stronger my brother". Uriel" Yes, Thanks for noticing". Uri "Watch this is the move I used to capture leviathan. Uri drew his spear and drew horizontaland vertical lines of lightning and hurled it toward ralph shot out green fire from his hands creating a shield of fire blocking aries attack. As to two moves collided a shockwave went out. Haniel a red headed angel warrior with orange flaming wings like mike, wielding dual flaming swords in her hands. Clade in gold and orange armor with a bit of white mixed in. Long flowing hair swaying flames shimmer al around her. Her sister Costello who is always by Haniels side, A blonde beautiful angel with white feathery wings clade in gold and white armor, wielding a bright sword of light. She also has power to control wind with her wings. Costello says "Hey Sis ready for sparing?" Hannah "Yeah but we arent sparing each other". Costello "no?" Hannah "We are dualing Sophia and Jophiel". Costello "oh". Sophia was one of the most beautiful yet powerful Arch - angels she has elegantly long black silcky hair, pink flaming wings, Pink and gold armor , or a flowing pink dress. Sophia wields a pink flaming tranangular sword that she can use to trigger a force field that not even a hypersonic missile can penitrate. Jophiel is a bold powerful Arch-Angel who grows in power the more she sings to God. She has one wing of fire and another of ice she has purple tights and silver armor. Jophiels sword is like her half fire and and ice, she can launch a shockwave of ice and fire. She can also shoot her powers from her hands. She has a beautiful kinky-fro. The time had come for these sisters in arms to test their skills. Haniel and Costello readied Sophia and Jophiel readied, BooooM Haniel" We're going to win, Costello "yeah but don't get too confident" Sophia/ Jophiel they aren't ready , jophiel "nope". Hannah and Costello slash toward Sophia an Jophy. Jophy blockers the attack with her sword, chinggggg! Sophia shout stunning hannah! Costello counter with a wind attack and haniel shoots fire creating fire-nados blasting sophia and jophiel back.

Jophiel "Wow that fight was epic we are amazing!"

Hannah "Yeah you really tested my resolve"

Sophia "That's the important thing to improve our skills and see were are weaknesses are".

Costello "Your too smart Sophia, all in all another great sparing session". "I know we'll be ready when the time comes".

Esther a very powerful Chinese Arch-Angel Clade in Red and gold armor wielding a red or green and gold guan dao. Her wings blaze fiery red and crackle with thunderous sounds as she flies through heaven. Esther "I was practicing swinging my guan dao and instructing my troops". "I missed the sparing oh man".

Jophiel "I'll spare you" Esther "Ok thank you, sister". Esther Drew her guan dao and swung it towards Jophy ,slashing jophiel. Jophiel strikes back with a ice attack cooling her flames. Then the two battle intensely until injury. To prove a point training mus be as real as possible, the fallen ones aren't going to go easy nor a horde of demons. Raphael came as the medic and healed their wounds. Jophiel and Esther "laughed" hahahahah "Now that was something and the bowed to each other. Mike Cammanded "ok, sparing is over, we all learned a lot in this exercise now we must go and ready our troops at once"

During all of this a saraphim burning one was watching and wanted to learn how to use her power to fight. Ena Katsumi asked Jophiel "how is she so powerful"?

Jophiel replied, "I worship the lord always, I pray pray pray, and The lord strengthens me."! "Bless his holy name!" Jophiel shouted. Ena "Thanks for the tip Sister". Ena started to practice she already sings and worships around God's throne, but she needs to focus that energy to fight.

CHAPTER 2

Get Ready

Be sober, be vigilant; because your adversary the devil, as a roaring lion, walketh about, seeking whom he may devour - 1 Peter 5:8

Blessed is the nation whose God is the LORD, the people he chose for his inheritance. - Psalm 33:12

PRESIDENT ETHAN BLACKWELL AND VICE PRESIDENT GARRET MORGAN OF AVALARIA

The nation of Avalaria prepared for a massive celebration, but this is momentous event was a massive W for all of humanity. After hundreds of years the 888th year of victory over Satan. President Ethan Blackwell and Vice President Gerett Morgan joined the Congress and Supreme Court. In a Massive Celebratory parade led by The Setinel Forces of Avalaria or

The capital city of Avalaria Avalard

(SFA). Millions gathered in the capital Avalon City to cheering and waving flags. The Airforce zoomed across the skies with thousands of aircraft from transport planes to advanced fighter jets and drones, Displaying avalaria's air dominance. Off the coast, Huge cruise missile destroyers, frigates, aircraft carriers, Amphibious Assault Ships, and other naval vessels. Sail in naval an armada outside the parade. The hearts the the citizens swelled with national pride for their country. 300,000 troops marched in the parade. The technological advancement had given rise to a whole new sector of Avalaria's forces Space Guardians. They had laser guns, Attack space jets, and specialized combat and galactic protective suits made for -10,000 to 7000 Ferienhiet. The suit were also resistant to blunt drama and stabproof. These guardians flew in earth's upper atmosphere streaking between the first and second heavens the Earth and outer space. The Space Guardians were ready to confront any threat to the planet. The victory parade broadcast globally through television an social media billions watching world wide. Other nations held similar celebrations in solidarity for humnitys victory over evil. President Blackwell Spoke "Good morning, my fellow Avalrians, Centuries ago a Supernatural entities threaten the very survival of humanity and our beloved home we call earth, the hatred and malice that these creatures showed was despicable, the murderous rampages, leaving millions dead. The level of untold destruction not only to our infrastructure by the eco-system was unfathomable. Through all of this humanity came to together politically,militarly,and socially to face this demonic threat, dispite our differences in politics and beliefs. We didn't cowar and hide or surrender but against all odds we fought and won. It needs to be said that without the help of God and his Heavenly Host we may have not survived the fight. Not only did Heaven help us puch back the demonic threat but also They dispensed Judgement on those responsible. We will be forever grateful to God, Jesus, and the Holy Spirit for fighting for us. The world is not fair but god did not forsake us despite our sins, He is worthy to be praised, faithful, and just is he the Lord of Hosts. I need to address a major disappointment: some of us have betrayed humanity and aided the Lord of Darkness in his fight against God's most prized creation. Make no mistake it hasn't been perfect their has been other wars and uprisings but nothing like the great Demon war Centries ago. I want be clear to any future advisaires ,Should another war arise and collaborators will be brought to justice swiftly. Happy 888th Victory Day, November 1, 2888. May The lord bless, Keep us, make his face shine upon us and, continue to grace us with peace, and protect us from evil. God Bless The Earth. Vice President Gerett Morgan Added "Although we have had peace for long we must remain viglant in order to Show strength to future enemies. As the Celebrations winded down, people went on happily with their lives, marrying, partying, and working. Not worrying about any new threats, putting faith in the ASF. Far away on the beyond earth on the planet Jupiter Lurks an Ancestral Power a mighty chief fallen Angel called Asmodeus a brother of Satan himself. Asmodeus is the most powerful of the fallen angel ancestral principalities ranks. He is inside the planet Jupiter in the thick clouds of ammonium, hydrogen, and helium with flashes of blue lightning all around. He is a huge blue-skinned, muscular Angel. His wings are covered in this light brown mixture of gas, and the gas swirls around him. He wields a big mace that he uses the call the most powerful blue lightning strike in the universe, 6x more powerful than Earth's lightning. He also shoots the toxic gas from his hands. He settled here after God commanded the Arch-Angels to expel the rebels from heaven into the dark void of the universe. Asmodeus has been plotting his revenge for millennia he is a very vengeful being. He knows soon the seal over his brother's kingdom will released, and this time, he won't stand idly by and watch heaven and insignificant human beings attack his kin. He was once a powerful Arch-Angel a near pear adversary of Micheal. He is one of many Ancestral Powers throughout our galaxy and beyond. Asmodeus Scoffed "They should have chained us to huh? It's so hahaha They are going to wish that did, haha. I will suck the life from those pathetic bags of flesh, or should I zap them with my lightning strikes"? hahaha, the time is approaching ready or not here we come!

GENERAL ALEXANDER STORMHEART OF THE SENTINEL FORCES

Suddenly the earth shakes for about thirty minutes people bang to pack but it was short-lived few knew what had just happened. In the coven, the sorcerers celebrated as they knew what the earthquake meant. They begin to dance, chant, and burn candles with incense to BAAL. In the Abyss "Finally We are free", Satan said relived to his wife Satana and Son the lawless one (antichrist). The anti-christ spoke "I can finally deceive people again it's what do best haha those stupid humans always fall for our tricks". "That's my boy", Satana said as a proud mother. "I will make them pay for what they did to my Children they won't survive this time I swear on my throne as Queen the abyss"! Satana Shouted angrily blood boiling as a mother with a hurt child. The demons and evil ones were catching their breath and gathering their thoughts, after being imprisoned in the abyss without freedom of movement for more than eight centuries. Satan ordered the anti-christ to gather hell's best for the meeting in hells gathering square. "Yes, Father of Darkness as you command" The anti-christ replied. Lilith "I'm finally un-bound yess, I am so going to hurt every one above ground for this!" she yelled like a spoiled brat. Jezebel unchained "hey lilith glad to see you again big sis, we are going to have so much fun kicking but in this next war i've had so much time to think of how to trick and hurt people haaaahaaa,"Jez sneered. Python a Giant snake slithered out of his cage, "Hey girls you too are already chatting it up huh, ugh my snake bones are all stiff I need stretched out" crack, crack,Python joked. Bak'tor "mooed", and stretch as he picked up a axe with molten lava. I'm gonna slay 1,000 warriors with these, I've practiced in my head haha," Bak'tor Joked. Belial skirted out of his lizard trap cell walking toward Bak'tor, "Where's Beezubulb," Belial questioned. "I'm right here", Beezulbub Replied. "A more scrawny than the rest aye and ugly my eyes," Belial teased. "Shut up Before I swarm you with insects Belial", "I Love eating insects I'm a lizard humanoid demon haha", Belial snapped back. Beez yelled "Lizard eating insects"! "Don't be so sensitive Beez just joking" Belial replied "Whatever bro "Beez" replied as he they walked toward the assembly square. Aberdeen a giant red dragon stood up, shaking loose his chains "Rooooooar , Micheal will pay for chaining me down here and slamming me into the ground", and humanity will be in fear just at the sigh of me, that sounds like fun rooooooar"! Aberdeen spake proudly. Leviathan breathed through his gills fresh sea water "sighed", I'm free, I thought I'd never get free, "People should drown in depths of the ocean for daring to attack me the Greatest fish in sea Levithan, Who is like me "? Leviathan shouted pridefully. The lawless one sent out a telepathic alert to gather in Hell's Assembly Square. Levi Peerd through the window to the meeting square, awaiting Satan's orders. All the demons and possessed humans ran full speed into the assembly square. The Dark Lord began to speak, "Welcome citizens and soldiers of The Abyss, I Would like to begin by Taking responsibility for our defeat, I've had time to think it through. We can inflict maximum damage on God's creation of mankind, not by willy-nilly attacks and rage. We were way too overt last time, we need to plan and prepare to stay under the radar and not raise suspicion. I task the demons with building weapons and armor and practicing fighting with each other, to form a well-trained demon army. To my Demon chiefs deploy to the underground base at the Scorched Sands Stronghold the desert from the last war you planned and strategize from there it can also serve as a weapons factory to eclipse soldiers and build up a physical army to get your revenge. There are other Eclipse soldiers who went undercover after surviving the war they aid you. "Commander Lord Malphas Darkbane you will lead my Eclipse army," Satan Commanded. "I do have really strengthening news we have allies in the second heavens waiting to assist, They have all ready been training and arming for this war they stayed out of the last war to prep for this future war"! "Lilith and Satana cast a stealth spell so our agents of darkness remain undetected." "Yes Sir", Satana, lilith, and jezebel agreed! We aren't alone going complete your task I'll be in touch remember rewards are waiting", Satan ordered!

JIM THE MILITARY SCIENTIST

The demon's began welding their weapons and training in the abyss. The demon began reinforcing the abyss with steel barriers and defensive attack positions. The original crew went under cover of night on a full moon into the bunker base in the Scorched Sands Stronghold. Bak'tor, Belial, Beelzebub, Python, Jezebel, Lilith, Snow Beast Guardian, and Demon Judas. Began developing attacks on humanity and contingency plans if the church or Sentinel spe-ops engaged them. The Evil ones are playing catch-up on the back foot. "All right ladies and gents, I don't know how much we will need to make it but, We need as much equipment and weapons as we can produce so get to it!" Lord Malphas Darkbane Shouted at the troops. There was still a lot of good old equipment and weapons there from the last war in good condition because the ASF didn't secure the bunker after the Battle of Sizzling Sands centuries ago. The soldiers were glad to have guns, tanks, helios, drones, ammunition, artillery systems, air defense, missiles etc.The eclipse forces would still need much more and their is a R&D lab under the base to advance their tech. A Soldier asked lilith "How did they miss all this"? "I started a distraction… read book one lol", Lilith joked. The soldier's began weapons production at a breakneck pace. Aberdeen and Levi await orders to deploy. The R&D was made for advancing weapons tech but it never came about in an active war. The first operation kidnap a military scientist. Four eclipse spec-ops catch a scientist on the way to his car. He fights back but is subdued the bring him back undetected and force him to give military tech secrets to Eclipse R&D. So Far things going according to plan.

ABERDEEN IN THE ABYSS

CHAPTER 3

Rolling Thunder

For we wrestle not against flesh and blood, but against principalities, against powers, against the rulers of the darkness of this world, against spiritual wickedness in high places. - Ephesians 6:12

Avalaria a few months later launched its annual military drill on February 7th, this year drills are called "Exercise Pheonix

Rising". The drill ordered by General Alexander StormHeart is to maintain readiness for any future Demon war it takes lessons learned from the first Demon war. A few allied countries joined in on the drill and pledged support to avalaria the drill covered ground, naval, air, and space warfare, preventing loss of life and damage to the planet. The drill was a success. Asmodeus sends a spiritual message to the whole kingdom of darkness in the abyss and throughout the galaxy {"We will entirely destroy the planet Earth, Arise oh Fallen Stars and destroy the earth"}! The two main planets activate operations. The first planet is a hot volcanic hellscape called Infernia. Infernia is a distant planet on the edge of our solar system. This planet is full of demons of all kinds and is much like the abyss. Infernia has huge cities and a demon society of anarchy working as a factory for demonic troops and weapons to aid the Dark networks in the second heaven. The second planet is called Xenovia. Right next to Infernia is Xenovia a beautiful pink and green looking planet. It's a lush planet full of alien plants and animal life. Xenovia is also home to many advanced alien species, who live in high-tech cities and have a counsel government, armed forces, and Politics. Greys, Draconians, Xenorians, Infernians, Nebulans, and Palladians are the main aliens that live on these planets. The Greys, Draconians, Nebulans, and Palladians are from far-off galaxies. These Groups of aliens each have different motives. The other lords across the solar system readied their power for the day of battle. The complete Operation Falling Stars plan was delivered by satan "This is how we will destroy them the fallen angels we must try to prevent the main Arch-Angels from focusing on the operations of the the demons on earth. Each ancestral power will distract the Chief angels for as long as possible, if all else fails the powers can use their powers to destroy the planet Earth and all humans from existence. We will need to attack separately so were all won't get defeated,"Satan gives the marching orders. Every demon and Fallen Angel salivated at the thought of revenge and victory over good and righteousness. After nine months of preparedness by all sides, the first shots of The Second Eternal Battle were about to begin! Jesus is handed a scroll of judgement on Satans new military aliance. Jesus "Micheal and the heavenly hosts The adversary and several Fallen arch-angels have hatched a conspiracy against my creations, they seek to destroy my favorite planet and Creation mankind. I'm giving you a blank check Micheal and the heavenly resources you need and as many angels as it takes! The foolish arrogant rebels plan must be averted at all cost go now fight for Heaven and The Lord of Hosts! Micheal and his angels bowed and saluted their commander and flew out of the gates of heaven toward a swirling black hole a portal into the natural realm. A Multitude of Heavenly Hosts dispersed throughout the universe clad in power and light. The angelic Generals assigned combat roles to the angelic forces. Some of the angles were to assume human form to carry out Secret missions. This division was headed by the aspiring warrior seraphim Ena Katsumi HIA a new recruit getting a shot to show her skill in real operations working in the Heaven Intelligence Agency. Other angels were assigned to protect people and regions . The rest of the angelic force are soldiers of various ranks from micheal down to the lowest ranking soldier. They headed toward our galaxy noticing the highly complex demonic network that had been established. This network is called the "Neabule Nexus", a system like this will complicate the mission tremendously. The angels faced a dilemma focused on the Neabule nexus and risk many human lives that could have been prevented or focus on earth and risk the solar system falling into chaos. Micheal we'll need to split up to tackle this nexus and preserve human lives. I will go after Asmodeous he's the leader of this nexus and the most powerful. Gabriel you go after Baal he dwells in the asteroid belt. Raphael you pursue Azrech "The Heartless" on the frozen wasteland of Pluto. Haniel you pursue Esheth "Godess of Sin" on venus. Uriel, you go to Mercury to fight the twins Al'gid, and Ral'gis. Jophiel, Costello, Esther, and Ena go to earth and buy us time and do your best to protect the people and fight the Demons. "Remember your not alone if you feel overwhelmed, you can call on many legions of angels to assist you, I believe in you all you showed tremendous skill and courage in the last "Eternal Battle", and now you'll make easy work of these already defeated foes the

Lord is with you! Micheal reminded and encouraged them. On earth breaking news about a missing military scientist who had a top secret clearance. The public wasn't so interested in the story but President Blackwell was very nervous. The man jim was last seen exiting a military lab and walking to his car when he never returned. General Stormheart de-brief the president "Hello Mr. President, the disappearance of this military R&D scientist is bigger than we first thought it appears he was one of the top military developers in our entire Army Sir, If that classified info gets out to our enemy it would be a major nation security threat"! President " how does a top scientist just disappear one day"? I don't know sir but based on a preliminary investigation by Captian Wells we believe he may have been kidnapped by highly trained personnel". "Find him them then"! The president ordered, "Yes, sir" I'll get Captain Wells on it ASAP! General Storm Heart. Two days later Captain Wells spec-ops team retraces Jim's steps. "It seems there's some blood by car on the ground from a struggle, let's test it"? "It's a match his DNA is on the ground he kicked one of the attackers and broke their nose". Soldier said. Then the soldier froze eyes wide "no ,no,no ,no way , "It's possessed demonized blood the, "Stop, Playing around", the team said. As the Lord lives this is tainted blood. "Ok we believe you", the team replied. Captian "We have a problem demon blood has been found". I assumed as much since the perps hadn't been caught", I've got to warn the president that they are back. "Mr. President the possessed demonized soldier kidnapped jim they may already have all the classified info they need by now," Captain Wells reported. President Blackwell and vice president morgan meet with the generals and captain Wells team. "We never thought this day would come again but another demon war possibly worst than the last is upon us, the only good thing is that we have invested in military preparedness the last 888 years. We've learned a lot from the last war

LORD MALPHAS DARKBANE GENERAL OF THE ECLIPSE ARMY

And God won't fail us I'm authorizing an offensive by executive order against Eclipse Forces. "This could be a mistake they still don't know that we are aware yet and the people and Congress aren't going to like this" General Stormheart warned. "They won't like getting Deleted by demons either , I was elected to protect the people and make the tough choice this what we must do",! "What classified project was Jim working on the Angel project, it's a classified program to create robotic angel-demon killing machines after the first eternal battle the angel's courage inspired us to create something like them to fight any future demon threat". I hope he doesn't give up that secret. "We need to mount a rescue mission" cleared. The eclipse forces were already done with Jim and moved him to an outpost in Duskmire Hollow Forest. Captain Wells's elite team approached stealthy taking out eclipse soldiers. They finally found Jim. "what this is too easy they must have set him loose in order for us to find him. Let's look for evidence and search the bodies and any thing that looks like intel. I found some sand-scorched sands stronghold possibly". "Jim where did they take you? "it was there". Jim replied" Jim said. "They snatched me walking back to my car,I fought but they subdued me. "You broke one of their noses that's pretty awesome. "Oh did I nice" Jim said proudly. Did You leak classified info yes on weapons productions but none of our top-tier projects like Angel 1', they would have killed me. "I understand," Wells. "In all, I do have good news we were putting the finishing touches and simulations. These weapons can be fitted with 50cal. Guns, rocket launchers, flame throwers, and Jetpacks. "That's Great prepare that and any other secret projects that could help us win a supernatural war" President Blackwells said. General Stormheart we should bait them into attacking we have a outpost near scorched sand stronghold." "OK, Stormheart and Wells I'm trusting you to take charge don't disappoint me". to the charge don't disappoint me" "We won't sir", Stormheart and Captain Wells said in sync. After the the meeting Wells and his team led by General storm heart deployed to Sandstorm outpost to begin probing operations. Captain Wells team of seven tier 1 operators and other marines were reselute and held and unwaviering commitment to defeating the enemy. These troops have no fear and not only trust in thier training and gear but The lord of Hosts! The ASF sent a message to the scorched snads stronghold to ask for peace. They sent the message on a unencrypted line. A Eclipse soldier recivied the message and rushed it to Lord Malphas Darkbane his Commander asap. As the soldier ran in the backgroup the base was a buzz the sounds of factory machines producing weapons and workers moving and testing miltary equitment. Ammunition, tanks,missiles, rockect, drones, helicopters, fighter jets, and advanced weapons systems being produced and stocked in inventory at a tremendous speed. The soldier finally reach the commanders office "General darkbane I have a message, The Sentinel force's have discovered our kidnapping of their scientist and they have located our base and are asking for peace", "I will have peace with sentiel force never only war, you've done well in forming me soldier i'll premote you, as for the soldiers who did the sloppy kiddnaping have them executed in front of the other soldiers as a warning. No games are being played anyone who fail's and compromises our mission get's killed!" Lord darkbane commanded The soldier was excited about his premotion but was a bit uneasy about his fellow soldiers being excecuted. He sent a message of rejection of peace and war declaration to the Sentinel forces base. Then he gives the other officers the orders to arrest and execute the spe-ops sodlier for getting detected. The eclipse soldier's stop their work and gather in the general area as Lord darkbane arrives grizzly and evil swirled around him courrupted by cheif regional demons and time in the abyss. "I know this is a unforgettable situation but I don't forgive screwups, you soldier's coprimised our operational security and must die as you know their is no mercy in the kingdom of darkness Praise BAAL"! Bang Bang Bang Bang Bang Bang! The whole team as shot by Lord Darkbane as a example. Then as if nothing happened the eclipse soldiers returned to working. Lord DarkBane went to inform The other Demon Lords from Baktor to Lilith. Clap,Clap, Clap the Demon lord welcomed Lord darkbane with aplause and praise, "Terrific job killing those idiots "Jezebel congratualatioly said grinning. "Ha,ha,ha it's nothing I have something serious to say", Darkbane laughed "We have been detected against satans wishes" I will answer to him. LordDark band approached Satan throne and confessed. " I respect you fessing up that's very brave nothing will happen to you because you killing them apeases my my anger". Satan said "Yes, My Lord It won't happen again". Lord Darkbane Satana sent him back to the base using abyss majic. "We are about to launch a attack on their base get ready", "Roder that" the Soldiers repeated. "The work and patience you have given will be rewarded I know your bone's are itching to get revenge on those so called Sentinels". Lorddarkbane cheered. Captain Wells received the Formal war declaration. "Wow they are way more formal this time", Wells said laughed. "Commander we need to call the president" wells said "ok"stormheart. Ring,ring,ring, "Hello Mr. President Blackwell, stormheat said.

"What's happening?,President. "Sir, The eciplse soldiers responed to my peace preposal with a declaration of war"Stromheat "Hit, em You are cleared to engage , I'll rally he allies. "President Blackwells said. "We'll let them hit us first". General stormheart ordered. Whoosh ,Whoosh two ballistic missiles were fired toward Sentinel Forces Sandstrom Outpost, BOOM,BOOM, two massive shockwaves rocked the base the gound shook for 20 seconds. The Sentinel soldiers readied their defenses "Don't fire yet," Stormheart cautioned. The Eclispce forces readied a massive attack embolded by the lack of response. Salvos of missiles and artillery, tanks began rolling toward the base jets went airborne firing toward The SandStorm Outpost. Boom,Whhooosh,whooooosh,Boom, the base took massive hits and damage as the soldiers took cover awaiting orders to return fire make no mistake General StormHeart knows what hes doing baiting their attack. "Hold the Line , Hold, Hold Fire" Gen. Stormheart! Ballistic missiles soar across the sky at hypersonic speeds, air defences activate and intercepting incoming missiles and artillery. Crusie missile desroyers fire salvos of cruise missiles Crush the Eclipse attack. The eclispse forces Pop a smoke screen and evacute the base retreating with most of the equipment they preduced for war. Once they fully emptied the base they went to set up a new base in the Forest region of Avalaria. Many Eclipse soldier's died hundreds no time morn the wicked don't rest. The Sentiel soldier approched the scrochsands stronghold in armored vehicles, tanks and on foot when sudden boom mines were struck killing a 12 Sentinel marines. The remaining troops entered the base throung a thick heavy steel door. A vast underground base with barracks, weapon production faclities war room and deep long tunnels was revealed the Sentinel soldiers began taking over the base and investigating the R&D research lab to gathered intel on their full capability and future plans.They found war plans for attacks on civilians , the capital Avalara, other nations, and the churches. The strangest thing of all wars strange evil smell that lingered, the smell of demons in the abyss burning sulfur. From this day forward the balance of peace was now offset and war had returned after hundreds of years of relative peace. The people of Avalaria and the church would not fear no matter what is coming trusting in God always nobody said life was going to be easy and no one would get hurt.

President Blackwell and Vice President Morgan in addition to General Stormheart gave a speech to announce the new war. "My fellow avalarians and the broader global community the event that have transpired over the last few months are troubling, a military scientist was kidnapped by Eclipse forces, Then Eclipse forces attacked our base after offering peace we counter - attacked killing hundred's but they retreated ,unfortunately we lost a dozen soldiers appoching the base. It appears another Demon war is now upon us. Do not fear we have prepared long for this day investing in our military strength for the defence of of humainty along with our alllies we will fight till the last blade edge for our survival as we did before,"President Alexander Blackwell. " We will be victorious against the devil and we'll push him back every chance we get "Submit yourselves to God.Resist the devil and he will flee"(James 4:7) Vice President quotes to encourage the people. "Our forces have already given a swift defeat to this evil army and if they want more they will get more and we'll send them back to the abyss permanently", General Stormheart Roared! The peoples hearts were anxious about what comes next but they were ready to fight for a future were humans exist.

CHAPTER 4

The Righteous and Wicked

The LORD is gracious, and full of compassion; Slow to anger, and of great mercy. The LORD is good to all: And his tender mercies are over all his works. - Psalms 145:8-9

Let no one be found among you who consigns a son or daughter to the fire, or who is an augur, a soothsayer, a diviner, a sorcerer, one who casts spells, or one who consults ghosts or familiar spirits, or one who inquires of the dead. - Deuteronomy 18:10-11

For since the creation of the world God's invisible qualities—his eternal power and divine nature—have been clearly seen, being understood from what has been made, so that people are without excuse. - Romans 1:20

The heavens declare the glory of God; the skies proclaim the work of his hands. Day after day they pour forth speech; night after night they reveal knowledge. - Psalm 19:1-2

The Church was a place beauty and glory where Gods glory was felt more than any other place on earth. For unbelievers, they wouldn't understand as without faith you can't tap into spiritual things. As the empending escalation war approached the Prophetic councel prayed ,fasted, and anointed themselves consicrating themselves to God. The Saints know this battle isn't is more than flesh and blood but spritual. Some saint's do take up

arms but they only use it in a righteous way for defense of their families , community and the church. In such a unstable situation the people of God would not fear but put faith in the power of The Lord of Hosts. He is worthy of all praise , honor, and glory. God is faithful and just in his judgments. The saints of Christ sang to God, Jesus,and the Holy Spirit songs of worship and praise for the blessing they had given, wisdom, understanding, and sustaining them through life's many battles. One such battle would be like none other and every challenge they have overcome

LILITH THE WITCH

up until this point has prepared them. The Miricle of The Two Eternal Prophets was a testament that with God, anything is possible. One the Leaders of the Prophetic counsel spoke. "Satan once again has risen up to try to destroy us, but the spirit of the lord will rebuke him, The Angels have been given charge to protect us some of us may die physically but spiritually, you will live forever if you repent of your sin's and believe in Jesus Christ and Obey Gods word. The Devil all so has his servant's, the sorcerers of the coven, They seek to break our connection with God. They want to steal what belongs to us, they're wicked and most of all they want us to suffer or be dead. They use all kinds of majic and other forms of witchcraft to hurt us, but God has given us power through Jesus Christ and the Holy Spirit. Know this: we will prevail! Back in the Coven at the Frost Peak Fortress, the news of the demon's return to Earth has spread the Soceres are elated that their queen Lilith is possibly coming back. The new coven is beautiful Stone and Marble and a Long flight of stairs atop a beautiful mountain with thick crunchy snow a real winter wonderland. The witches layed out purple and scarlet decorations, a long purple carpet like that of british royalty. The window's were mulitcolored stained glass. The witches robes were more colorful bright and pretty. Their evil atlers and culdrons decked out an ready for also any spiritual warfare, spell, hexes, and other dark arts of witchcraft. The male sorserors wore purple and wizard robes with a pentgram on the chest. The most important articles in the temple of evil were the idols. The sorserers didn't just us spells and majic they worship the ancestral spirits, fallen angels ,and demons. They dance, chant, and pray for more evil spirtual power to fight for satan.The members of the coven cult also worship water, the earth, trees, and The stars in addition to using wood,dirt,sand,air,moon and the sun to cast spells. They believe that because they work for satan he will give them a job after they die and go to the abyss. They are just useful idiots in satans war agianst humanity and tratiors of their fellow man, working to block and stifle peoples progress instead of helping their fellow mankind. The anticipation reached a fever pitch as the Coven awaited Lilith and Orpheus the original founder of the coven a powerful wizard as wicked as they come hardened from time in the abyss. The Coven's hearts beat in creased as their spiritual senses tingles filling the power of their Queen an King approach. The massive marble stone door slowly opened wide. The Sorcerers bowed as lilith and Orpheus entered the wicked Temple. They cried in awe and reverence of Witch of Witches and The Warlock of Warlocks entered the Coven. Orpheus Spoke " Hello every one this place is amazing, I would first like to congratulate our newest members for re-building our Coven. Everyone who was involved will get a special charm of madalin infused with the power of the abyss." "Yes, all of my loyal sons and daughters will be rewarded for your dedication, I'm back from the abyss we were defeated but now we rise from the ashes of the abyss to carry on the struggle against the people of God and That theocratic government"! Lilith announced" "Woooooo", the crowd roared with excitement. Not only had Lilith and Morpheus returned but those who were in hiding after surviving Gods wrath against the Wicked. The Coven cult ate goat meat, and drank red wine in a great celebratory feast detcicated to Baal. "Where's Jezebel," a witch asked? Lilith Aswered "She couldn't Join us today unfortunately because she has other work to do for our war efforts". "I miss her". "You'll see her soon enough" Lily replied the next day Orpheus gathered everyone into the arena connected to back of the coven. Tens of thousands gathered experience and recruits to learn the dark arts and how to use majic to attack people. Orpheus touch the ground picking up hard crumbly dirt tossing it into the air and blowing it the dirt turned into viscous flying scorpion like insects. The cult members were so impressed clapping. Next he shot flames from his hands surrounding himself in flames but he was not burned. "The crowd shout it's the power of the abyss wow Baal is amazing"!Orpheous the wicked then lifted his rigged staff toward the sky ask the prince and power of the air to to extinguish the flames an rain poured. Orpheus wasn't done yet he then held his madalen called a spell to make a illusion of multiple clones. Lastly Orpheous is hit his staff on the ground and a 6.6 magnitude earthqauke was triggered. "What I have Just Deminstrated was a small taste of what one can due if he or she wants to jion the dark side and sell their soul to the abyss and forfeit heaven". The wizard spoke. The crowd sat silent some were unsure fully committing to evil. Lilth now bagan a demonstration shooting her famous pink ad green flames creating a huge ring of pink and green fire floating above the abyss the pulled the fire down creating two pillars of fire. The crowd cheered in shock at the level of her power she the turned her fire into weapons and summoned a large demon beast and slayed it after a hard fought battle. "To all of my children you can see our power is beyond any limits she lied, Forget the failures of the past a practice your craft together we can do significant damage to Sentinel and the church. "We will win by the Power of

Baal" the wicked cult shouted. One the warlocks shouted "Can you make bigger pillar of fire"? "Yeah,"Lily giggled She sent telepathic messiage to Aberdeen to help with a Spell. "I got you Sister, I'm ready for some action " Aberdeen swiftly soared from

ORPHEUS THE WIZARD

the abyss Sentinel scrambled jets but the he disappeared of the radar. The pilots reported a ufo to command and flew back to Sentinel HQ. Aberdeen approached the upper stratosphere of the earth reading his powerful flames. Lilith side it said in that book that their God can spanned a pillar of fire for a ancient prophet elijiah, well we can do that to our pride is too strong", Lily Blasphemed against the Lord of Hosts.By the power of the abyss ,"I call down fire from the Second Heavens", and Aberdeen spewed a powerful stream of thick fire onto to a bare tree which didn't burn like bibles story. The crowed said "truly she is a daughter of the abyss". Back at the church the spirit of the living

God moved powerfully in the beautiful sanctuary of holiness. The beautiful stained glass full of colors and the amazing limestone walls and elegant white and golden curtains, floors of pearl. They prayed in their white and golden robes praying in heavenly languages strengthening themselves and interceding for the church member, military ,government , fellow people ,nations and even coven member that those who haven't fully committed to Satan would turn from wickedness and accept Jesus Christ's Covering for sin. It's not God's will any go to the abyss but he gave us free will so our own action of rejecting God and righteousness and rebeling sends us to Judgement. The regular church member's wore beautiful suits, dresses, or nice causal clothes. The people of God repented of sins hungering for righteousness. They fasted, Healed people of aliment's ,cast out demons, anointed and blessed fellow christians. By the Power of the Holy Spirit and Jesus, and The Lord Rapha the healer, the miracles are delivered through the virtue angels. Every evil chain was uprooted in Jesus mighty Name and many people gave their lives to God. The church was flourishing but so were the evil ones. The church began to boast about Gods awesomeness, "God you alone are worth of praise and glory none can compare to you". "Even the Stars in Heavens sing your praises, the chirp of a cricket, the howl of a wolf, the roar of a lion and every creature you made worships you with their unique sounds." "The rushing waterfall a monument of your power Lord God." "The wind whistle of strong gust praises it's creator "By Thoughts and Words the universe and trillions of galaxies, stars and planets formed, they move according to your command and swirl and dance in praise to you across the second heaven!" 'Every molecule and atom vibrates to give glory day and night." "All creation was created to lift you high and praise your name So I Could Sing your name 100 trillion times"! "Who is like our God the only one and true living God,no one"? God you had mercy on humanity after we sinned against your will, You even sent your son of his own will to leave his throne in heaven, take on flesh and a body, and live a perfect life to show us how and give his life so we could have our sins forgiven and get to escape the abyss if we repent, then he went into the abyss confronted Satan, Satana, and The Lawless One took their rights over death they received after satan tricked adam and eve into sinning, No other have that kind of love." Blessing and honor and glory forever and ever. The choir began to sing Hallelujah 3x for the Lord God's almighty reigns, Holy, Holy, Holy. Amongst the choir was Costello in human form singing praises to the Lord. The church was blessed by her stunning vocales not knowing she was an angel among them. Costello was on a mission under cover from Micheal to watch over and protect the church since the other arch-angels has to stop massive powers in the second heaven. After the service Costello a beautiful blonde European angel with elegant feathers pure white wings, she wore gold and white armor. She was armed with a sword of light to fight evil, and she created whirlwinds and tornadoes to scatter evil. She overheard reports from another angelic spy that Eclipse had set up an HQ in the Forest and was planning attacks against the churches and several other locations. Costello met up with Jophiel , Ena and Sophia to discuss her intel and to strategize. "We need to be careful because we can't fight all of the demon lords without mike ,gabe, ralphs, or uri's help, were very strong but they have a lot more strength and power than we do, well need to prioritze tasks if theirs multiple attacks we'll lose a lot of people ,we won't be able to keep up let's consult Michael", Costello strategized. Then flew back to get direction from Micheal their commander. "We need some encouragement big Bro, we don't know if we have what it takes." Sophia spoke to Mike. Jophiel "Hey mike we need some direction how should we cover enough territory between us?" "first Well ena stay undercover with Sentinel forces and tip them off to aid you. Second Costello and Sophia you continue to watch the church when time comes you'll know what to do I believe in you. Third Esther you lay and back them up if they need it your combat skills are impeccable". I wouldn't have given you the task, I know it seems impossible but that's part of being hero and the truth is you can't save everyone but you just do best you can and give it 120%, you showed your skill at the end of The First Eternal Battle, you've got this if someone needs your help you girls should rescue them." "I'll give you'll some extra power hold my hand, the God who dwells between the cherubims grant your mighty Son's and Daughter's strength and power, and we won't doubt but believe in your name, we can do anything through God in Jesus mighty name we pray Amen"! "Amen", Ena , Jophiel, and Costello said. "I will aid the army as you say commander and when time comes for me to blow my cover God will lead me". Ena flew back to Sentinel HQ, returning to human form a beautiful Japanese woman spy. Costello and Jophiel also returned to earth to watch over the church now motivated and hopeful infused with more power from on high trusting not in their on might but in God's Spiritual power. In a very Short time the Eclipse army, working day and night had not only built a HQ to continue the work they started. They had begun to have bases in all the regions of Avalaria with highly trained soldiers equipped with offensive and defensive capabilities. Bak'tor Belial and Beezulbub had assembled demon armies and they spoke to Darklord Malphas about the integration of demon battalions to boost Eclipses' capability in the field "Alright but they must be held in check," Darkbane ordered. "Our demons know not to get out of line", Bak'tor replied.

The newly trained demonic battalions were deployed with Eclipse forces with their supernatural ability to deal with pain these minions armored up and armed with various weapons from claws to rocket launchers. It was now time to spilt up an take permanent positions. Jezebel and Python were the principalities ruling in the forest region Duskmire Hollow aided by their fairy an elf demons assisted by eclipse troops. Baktar, Belial, and Beezulbub regained their thrones in a new base now joined by demons made of sand, Lizard demons, Bull demons, incest demons and regular troops. The great snow Beast Guardian who once failed returned his frostpeak fortress, and now he had a new coven to protect and a vast army of demons made of snow. Aberdeen gathers his dragons to act as Satan's Demonic Air Force. Leviathan gathers a vast armada terrifying aquatic demons from his marine kingdom to war at and the coastland. Leviathan had grown tentacles on his back making him an even more powerful water dragon with powerful scales. New chiefs were appointed Bohemoth a huge powerful demon in charge of the ogre demon army sent just outside the city and Demon Judas having the form of and insane man who betrayed Jesus and his evil red demon form with incrusted rubies on his forhead symbolising his greed working to sabotage and betray the Sentinel army. God knowing the foolish pride of these rebels sent his second champion from ancient time the Samson a huge armored brute in golden armor with a cross symbol on the chest. Samson long hair lock's and massive muscles God's real life super human. "I'm no here to play no games, I failed last time never again, I'm ready to whoop any demon or soldier working against God will". Satan now with his troops in position sends a message to Xenovia and Infernia to get ready to aid and call up all reserve troops to back up those on earth. Infernia being a demon planet totally agreed. Xenovia some species of alien life were against fighting on earth only wanting defend their planet. The greys and draconian were the most eager to fight. Micheal and his angel's had been already fighting many evil being's trying to delay their operations to eliminate the Ancestral Spirits. Many angel lives had been lost in these battles but Mike, Gabe, Ralph, Uri, and Hannah fought on. They knew the only option was victory. Despite their will to fight through countless waves of enemies weighed on them heavely they grew tired bruised and battered their weapons and armor was truly tested. They endured knowing they are on a mission to complete no matter what nothing would make them quit. "How many more waves of enemies are there, I'll never quit"? Gabe sighed. "I must fight on creation depends on me beating Esheth", Haniel shouted. "I'll keep fighting , healing and reviving for as long as it take , I'm on a mission from God" Raphael Cheered! " I Take that you guys are tired ahh, I can do this all year, a little humour is needed in times like these right"?! Uriel Joked "The Lord is faithful our breakthrough is unstoppable, we are an unstoppable force look how far we've come", Micheal encouraged! Suddenly God Spoke "Not by Might nor by Power, but by my Spirit remember"! "Yes, we remember", they cheerfully replied. Suddenly a cosmic disturbance caused the fallen angel minions to retreat back to their planets. The Angels know took position prepping for hardest fights of their existence, know that the powers come from the Almighy. A year had past now back on earth Commander alexander stormheat briefed the president " I'm very shock given the events of last yearthere was only on ufo sighting. Despite the military expantion of the eclipse forces." "I know they are going to atttack but they keep delaying ". "maybe your intel is wrong general", President Blackwell? retorts "no mr. president Black well, It's right and when it happens it could be catastrophic! "We , decided not go on the offensive due to casualty risks and fear of escalation truly". "With all the time they've had we are dealing with a war that makes the other 3 look like cute picnis", Stormheart said. " What other 2 wars", Presidentblack well ? "That's right it's classified and sealed to because they happened during the relative peace era", General said regretfully. " Nevermind that keeps our troops on Defcon 2 alert level ready for full scale combat". President Blackwell ordered

THE NEW COVEN

"Yes, Sir, One advantage is that our nations freedom allows citizens to bear arms to protect themselves against criminals or foreign invasions so armed citizens will be able to put up some resistance were our Military and Police are lacking, we could prep lethal and non-leathal aid to help our people"! The General suggested. "That's true and We'll certainly get those care packages ready for airdrops. President Blackwell ordered. "One more thing a new intelligence agent named Ena Katsumi has showed alot of promise no one really knows were she came from, but she say's she has actionable intel that Eclispse are planning attacks against civilian targets with in days." President Blackwell informed General Stormheart "Ok, send her over to the HQ Mr. President". Ena is Ordered by the president to go see General stormheart in Sentiel HQ. "Miss Katsumi the president has spoken very highly of you, what role do you think is best for you being in the Avalaria Intelligence Agency and all?" "It's an honour to meet you General Stormheart , i'm a huge fan of those fighting evil ,it's what i've deticated my life to. I believe being a free angel is best so I can keep eyes on anything unusual on base or off and I have super powers", she said jokingly yet serious. "Haha ,that's great we'll need what ever we can get", the general chuckled "Do your super secret spy thing dismissed" The general ordered. "I won't fail you sir, I'm on a mission from God"! Katsumi said resolutely "That's what I like to hear Soldier", General replied! Ena Katsumi God's Beautiful Battle Star set off the watch over the HQ and the city not knowing were her mission would led her but she walked by faith in the true and living God.

As the impending Doom creeped ever closer The Arch-Angels Jophiel, Esther, Costello, and Ena Katsumi on earth missed worship in heaven and gathered to sing O Come O Come Emmanuel to the Lord "O come thou wisdom from on high, who orders all this mightily…" Their Worship of the Most High God a million times more beautiful than all our greatest choirs and vocalists combined. A real angelic praise team leading worship in spirit and in truth. As they sang The people around the city both believers and non-believer felt a a true peace and a feeling of God's love thrunough the Holy Spirit's presence the same dove that descended on Jesus flew around the capital allowing people to feel the Lords presence tangably. Most of the skeptic in their pride chalked it up to emotional responses from beautiful musicians. The God head trinity shed tears in their love for the lost souls blinded by the pride of life and their so called intellect seeing themselves as gods or the universe.

CHAPTER 5

Rage of the Damned

When the enemy shall come in like a flood, The Spirit of the Lord will raise up a standard against him. -Isaiah 59:19

As the week came to a end on a perfect summer day, a gentle breeze swept across avalaria and the surrounding nations. The sun was shining in all of it's brilliance a true marvel of God's creation one of trillions of star's dotted across the Second Heavens. People went to work , children went to school. Their were immaculate weddings and sumber funerals. Traffic was busy and heavy cars bumper to bumper honking horns and road rage out bursts. As the day whined down people headed home , while others went out to party at clubs or spending time with family and friends on a late friday night. Just before sun set as the festivities ended the power suddenly went out no lights, tv, refrigerator ect. People were very confused but very tired they checked the electric panel to try and reset the power, but to no avail. People gave up the troubleshooting the power and went to sleep. Saturday morning as people started their day people began to panic because the power was still off. Things began to get much worse cars wouldn't start. People went out in to the neighbor hoods and asking their neighbors if they had the same issues and everyone had no working electronics. Back in the presidental palace General Alexander Stormheart rushes into president blackwells office to inform him. "Mr. President we have power outages all over the continent, even some military equitment is malfunctioning"! "The thing is it's not a emp, we confirmed with space command sir. "We are blind" General Stormheart reported! "We don't know what is going on but we must be ready raise the alert level to Alpha Priority 1.

ARCH-ANGEL COSTELLO

Order Shadow Stalker to transmit the encrypted war messages to Captian wells" The President ordered. "Captian Wells this is

Shadow Stalker transmitting Alpha,Lima,Picnic,House,Alpha Break Pencil,Rodger,Iglu,Owl,Rodger,Iglu,Yankee", "Rodger that Shadow stalker message recieved" Captain well responded. "Team listen up Every Spec-ops squad has just been activated.

We don't know what the threat is but this is what we've trianed for, Why we signed up for the tier one operator job. It's gotta be Dark Lord Malphas Bring it in Team,, prepare to face the storm. We're the shield in the darkness, the sword against chaos. We stand ready to defend our nation with everything we've

ARCH-ANGEL JOPHIEL

got. Let's show them what were made of." Captain Wells Back in the Forest Dark Lord Malphas commander of the Eclipse army rallied his troops "Soldiers of darkness, heed my call! Today, we unleash the fury of our wrath upon our enemies. They shall tremble before the might of our forces, for we are the harbingers of chaos and destruction! Let the fires of war burn bright, and let no mercy be shown to those who dare oppose us. Forward, my loyal warriors, and let the world know the true meaning of fear!" Malphas Sedisticly encouraged. The soldiers replied Yes, My lord we shall make them pay. We are ready to commit war crimes"! "Lilth and the coven are helping us they have cast a powerful spell disrupting all electronics to cover our assault." Commander Malphas added. Instintaneously Eclpise troops fired thousands of missiles into cities across Avalaria and the region. Whoosh,whoosh,whoosh,whoosh as the missile whisle and streak through the air. The sounds of explosions and screaming people began to fill the air as people tried to take cover from the missiles barrage boom as missiles rianed down on communites and neighbor hoods of civilians. Homes and cars exploded fires broke out with thousands of people injured and hundreds dead. In the Avalaraian city capital missiles rained down like snow in the winter causing massive damage and an even more civilan and military casulties. The president wanted to speak to the people but he couldn't with no power and it would be safe for people to stay in one spot during this brazen attack of epic preportions. The Sentinel air defenses were off line do to the covens majic. Feeling angry and helpless against this attack General Stomheart Prayed unto the Lord God who dwells in heaven between the cheribums. He prayed "O Lord, in this hour of uncertainty and turmoil, I come before you with a heavy heart. As a military general, I feel the weight of responsibility upon my shoulders, yet in this moment of surprise attack, I confess my helplessness before You.

Grant me strength and clarity of mind to lead my troops with courage and wisdom. Help me to make decisions that honor You and protect those under my command.

Lord, be our shield in the midst of chaos, our refuge in times of trouble. Guide our steps and lend us Your divine protection as we navigate through the fog of war.

Give me the humility to acknowledge my limitations and the faith to trust in Your providence, knowing that Your will shall prevail.

May Your grace sustain us, and may Your mercy shine upon us, even in the darkest of hours. In Your holy name, I pray. In Jesus Christ name Amen."

The Lord Heard Alexanders prayer and looked on him with grace and wisdom. He counted him among the righteouss because of his faith and humbleness. He chose pray and believed God in the worst of times and not trust only his intellect but acknowledge The Lord instead of blame him or blaspheme him for the devils actions. What The General didn't know is that God had already answered his prayer before he even thought to pray. The Lord of Hosts had already sent angels to assist in his mission. The missile barrage had stopped and people began to receive medical treatment for their wounds and count the bodies. The Senteniel Comms network and some power had returned. Even

AIR FORMATION

undestroyed cars began to start up but the roads were severely damaged and had huge craters for miles also some bridges were hit. As the Nation started to catch it's bearing after the missile attack. Little did they know that was only the first wave. Eclipses newly built naval ships and submarines set out to sea. After that several Eclipse air force jets took flight. The fighter jets targeted Sentinel Military Bases across the country, now that some air defenses were on line the Sentinel forces manged to shoot down dozens of jet's and intercepted cruise and ballistic missiles fired by the eclipse navy dispite their effort Sentinel forces still took massive causilties in the thousands. As Power began to be restored the jets and ships powered up General stormheart thanked God for his mercy. Now Sentiel stood a fighting chance. Sentinel Jets, atttack helicopters, and naval group moved toward the fight for an offensive attack. Silver and black advanced aircraft. Loop across the sky shooting down each other craft. Explosions filled the sky as burning jets and choppers fell out of the sky and crashed. The Sentinel navy began firing toward the eclipse battle ships striking several and sinking them. At once Leviathan swiftly from the deep and causes a massive wave to hit the Sentinel vessels. The Ships began to sway violently causing the Salors to be tossed against the walls some ships tipped at a 90 degree angle but recovered. Several cruise missiles hit sentiel ships sinking some to the buttom of the ocean. The navy target the monstrosity that is Levi with turrets causing him to quickly dive he was still weak and hadn't regained his full power yet. Lilith back at the coven was ticked that her majic spells were interrupted allowing Sentinel to fight back. "My Spells! Foiled by mere prayers! This interruption shall not go unpunished!," Lilith raged! Lord Malphas congratulated his troops "Bravo, my infernal warriors! Your relentless dedication to darkness has brought us one step closer to our ultimate victory!"

He lead the demonic Eclipse army toward Avalaria crushing smaller weaker nations. As he approached he offered a preposition "President Blackwell ,Vice President Garret Morgan, General Alexander Stormheart ,Captain Wells, and Avalaría Surrender to our might, or face obliteration at the hands of our infernal legions." "My fellow citizens, today our nation mourns the devastating loss of thousands of innocent lives in a cowardly act of aggression. We stand united in grief and resolve against this heinous attack.

To the invading general who dares threaten us with annihilation if we do not surrender know this, we will never bow to tyranny nor cower in fear. We will stand firm in defense of our sovereignty and freedom.

Let it be known to all who seek to oppress us that we will not falter, we will not waver. We will rise from the ashes of tragedy stronger and more determined than ever before.

To our enemies, we say this, We will not negotiate with terrorists. We will not yield to threats. We will fight with every fiber of our being until justice is served and our homeland is secure once more.

May God bless our nation, and may He grant us the strength to overcome this darkness that has befallen us." Presidentials Spoke firmly

"My fellow soldiers, today we have endured a grave and unprecedented assault on our nation and our forces. The enemy seeks to break our spirit, to crush our will, but I say to you now we will not be defeated!

NAVAL FLEET

Though our hearts may be heavy with the weight of loss, our resolve remains unshaken. We stand as guardians of our land, defenders of our people, and we will fight until our last breath if need be.

To the tyrants who dare threaten us with annihilation if we do not surrender: know this, we will never bow to your tyranny nor betray our principles. We will fight with every ounce of strength and courage until victory is ours or until we meet our fate with honor.

SUBMARINE FLEET

Let them come with their armies and their weapons, for we will meet them on the battlefield with unwavering determination and unyielding resolve.

Remember our fallen comrades, and let their sacrifice fuel our defiance. For today, we fight not just for ourselves, but for the future of our nation and for the freedom of generations to come.

Stand tall, my fellow soldiers, for we are the bulwark against tyranny, the shield of our homeland. And together, we shall prevail!" General Stormheart Roared

"To those who threaten surrender, heed this warning: our resolve is unyielding, our determination unwavering. Surrender is not an option. We are the silent reapers of justice, and we will pursue you relentlessly until every threat is neutralized." Captain Wells

The People of Avalaria were inspired to hear courage from their leaders and focused their grief to defend their nation. Civilians dusted of their leagal firearms and lay in wait to avenge their love ones an neigbors. The Sentinel army dug trenches outside the borders and deployed every armored combat vehicle they had ready for battle do or die. Eclipse forces charged gunning down the border defences and entering the thousands of soldiers parachuting in. Systematically they attacked one base after another, one community after another deleting even more people. As the Eclipse force pushed further into the country they met stiff resistance from civilans blasting many eclipse soldiers in a brave act of defiance to evil. The Eclipse army grew angry that they had face such a insignificant group of ragtag civvies holding them back for hours with semi-auto rifles until more police and miltary forces arrived. The brave citizens were awared medals after being sent away from the front lines.

"Your bravery in the face of invasion has inspired us all. The courage of ordinary citizens defending their homeland is a testament to the indomitable spirit of our nation. Thank you for standing strong and fighting for our freedom." President Blackwell said, as he pinned the ribbons and draped the medals on the brave heroes.

The only buildings untouched were a few churches They had survived the onslot of attack due to The Arch-angel Sophia protecting the buildings with her forcefield powers. She had to make a spilt second decision and a ethical one to save church or save random buildings. Knowing the help food,water and medical servives the churc could provide she chose to save some churches. She felt sad she couldn't help everyone, she remembered Mike telling you can't always save everyone. Sophia had hope knowing Jesus died for their sins of many who died and they are now enjoying heaven. She was knew this would be one of many battles. She did what she could and thats what mattered. The Eclipse forces had been stalled by the reinforced defensive line of well trained Sentinel forces. The Dark Lord Malphas grew angry with his stalled invasion and Summond Bak'tor,Belial,Beezulbub The Demon Lords and their hordes of demons. General Stormheart saw the demons approaching and ordered his troops to retreat toward the capital because the soldier were not equipped with anti-demon weopons. The Sentinel soldiers reluctantly whithdrew systematically placing mines and traps the slow the advance of the Domonic horde. The Sentinel army began to deploy their holy fire wepons used in the Last Demon War Rockects,missilies ,flame throwers, Tank Shells,Glory light beams,and laser weapons. They also prepped the Secret new weapons developed by the most elite Sentinel military R&D scientists including Petra-sonic Missiles, Arch-Angel Mechs, new upgraded Laser with Air /Ground/Sea-based systems, Advanced Artillery systems, MLRS 4.0 Systems. As the Eclipse army advanced aided by their demonic allies, explosion's erupted as the Eclipse troop's tripped a large quantity of land mines. The mines managed to kill a forth of the invading troop a rare win for Sentinel who has been on the back foot since the start of the conflict. The eclipse troops wanted to turn back but Lord Darkbane said "you must sacrifice your-self for the cause." The demon began to reek havoc in The capital chasing people down and killing them. The demon used their super strength to destroy what was left of much the Infrastructure. The demons burst through walls to find people trying to hide. Amongst the chaos a child 6 year's of age went out to fetch water from a tank to bring back to his younger siblings as their parents were killed in the attacks. The young boy was very strong and believed in The Lord of Hosts, he parent's were in the gardens of heaven. As the boy saw a opening he be-lined to the water tank quickly filling it up. As he turned around a large demon tried to scare him `and his siblings. The boy was not afraid and reassured his younger sibling God would help them. "You Demons threatening my life Die in the name of Jesus". Suddenly their gaurdian angel appeared and swiftly slayed the demons. The Children praised the God of their deliverance. The angel also brought them food. As the demons rampaged on they came across a science university the student ran in disbelief as many of them were atheists or agnostic who didn't believe in the superantural. They were now faced with a life changing experience chased down by supernatural demons. Some the students were raised in Culture of God but rejected him. One girl remembered what her mom would say "No weapon formed against me shall prosper in Jesus mighty name"! The demon snarled at them as a warrior angel hovered above them. The demons fled fearing the angel. Some of the science student's in the class gave their life to Jesus Christ that day,while others in their pride chocked it up to coinsedence. The Sentinel Soldiers fought with all their might as all Hell was breaking loose literally in the capital of Avaland. They shot hundreds of artillery rounds infused with holyfire from micheals recipe. The explosions began wounding and killing many demons. The Sentinel army now employed tanks and armored vehicles to defend troops from being killed by demons. The sound tank fire roared the city like a sound of hope. They fired MLRs at large groups of demons killing hundreds. Sentinel then demploy fighter jets , helicopters ,and drone swarms against the hordes. The Jets striked across the sky conducting air-strikes on the demons aided by attack helicopters. Sentinel ground troops fired their guns and flame throwers killing many more demons. As Sentinel troops gave everything they were currently able to deploy the invaders continued to advance. The initial missile attack took out my Sentinels soldiers so the troops able to deploy were thin in the north of Avalaria. The soldiers began to notice there were a lack of Eclispe human troop all of the sudden. They didn't think much of it as they were fighting hordes of demons. As The demon chiefs approached the front line General Stormheart ordered a full retreat abandoning the capital Avaland. The troops ran for their lives unable to stop this supernatural force. Truly the Devil had come in like a flood. The army ,government ,and all civilians who could evacuated to a city south of avalaria. The second largest city Sancturia a Modern Sprolling city

The Economic capital of Avalaria now after the Defeat in the Battle of Avaland. Sancturia would become the new secondary capital for now. Hundreds of Thousands of troops were waiting with lots of medical aid for the wounded. Back in the The Capital Few remained Ena Katsumi was the last one left in the Sentinel HQ Metroplos Bastion. "I stand alone in the command center, the echoes of battle fading into the silence that now engulfs me. As the last of my brethren, I carry the weight of our failure heavy upon my wings. The demons have won this round, and I ache with the knowledge that I cannot yet unleash my celestial powers to turn the tide. Hidden beneath this mortal guise, I mourn the loss of my comrades and the inability to fulfill my duty as their protector. But even in my sorrow, I steel my resolve, for I know that my time will come to rise and reclaim what has been lost." Ena said sorrowfully as she wept. Katsumi gathered her composer knowing she can't just sit around and mop she prayed a blessing over Captian Wells Teir 1 Spec ops Team to avenge the righteous "May the wings of unseen guardians guide your steps, O valiant warriors of the shadows. May the light of righteousness cloak your deeds in secrecy as you move through the darkness. May your swords strike true, your arrows find their mark, and your hearts remain steadfast in the face of adversity. Go forth, blessed by the Heavenly realm, to bring justice to the unjust and peace to the troubled. In Jesus name Amen." Ena Katsumi, the angelic heroine, stands tall and resolute, her long silky black hair cascading down her back as she finishes her prayer, her purple and gold armor gleaming in the dim light. A purple silk scarf drapes elegantly over her shoulders and neck, adding to her regal aura. Her wings, ablaze with purple flames, spread wide behind her, and she grips her long, flaming sword with determination.

As she opens her eyes, she is met with the sight of her adversary—a dark angel of beauty, with dark hair, black flaming wings, and menacing black horns protruding from her forehead. A black feathered tail sways behind her as she wields a long-bladed switch glaive with deadly precision. Clad in black and gold armor and a warrior's robe, she exudes an air of dark elegance.

Without hesitation, the two angels engage in an epic battle within the abandoned military command base. Their swords clash with thunderous force, the sound reverberating through the empty corridors as they dance with deadly grace. Ena Katsumi's flaming sword meets the dark angel's glaive in a flurry of sparks, each strike filled with the intensity of their opposing powers.

The battle rages on, neither angel willing to yield to the other. Ena Katsumi's determination is matched only by the dark angel's relentless fury as they trade blow after blow, their movements a blur of speed and precision.

LEVIATHAN

But as the dust settles and the echoes of battle fade, only one victor emerges from the fray, her purple flaming wings unfurling triumphantly as she stands victorious over her fallen adversary. With a solemn prayer for her fallen comrads, Ena Katsumi takes her leave, her resolve unshaken and her spirit unbroken.

After Praying, she Swiftly flies to Sancturia the new command center of the Sentinel forces.

At the Church Costello, Jophiel Prepares to defend the church. Baktor The Bull god ,Belial Lord of Lizards, Beezulbub Lord of the flies, approches the church. Costello and Jophiel walk out side and confront the demon army as the Church prays inside, with the wounded fearing the worst. As the heavy oak doors of the church swing open, Costello and Jophiel step out into the dim light of dusk, their celestial radiance muted beneath mortal guise. Clad in armor woven from starlight and wielding blades forged in the fires of heaven, the warrior angels exude an aura of unwavering resolve.

With determination etched upon their faces, they stride purposefully towards the looming silhouette of the demon lord, who stands amidst the swirling shadows, a malevolent grin twisting his features.

The three villains, cloaked in the darkness of their malevolence, gather in a shadowy alleyway, their sinister laughter echoing off the grimy walls before them stands their adversary, a figure of courage and resilience, her presence a beacon of hope amidst the gloom.

"Well, well, well," sneers one of the villains, a twisted grin spreading across his face, "look who decided to show up. Did you bring your little band of heroes with you this time Johpiel?" Bak'Tor mocks.

His companions join in the mockery, jeering and taunting as they circle their foes like vultures closing in on prey.

"You're all alone now. Your new partners weak, darling," purrs another villain, a glint of malice in her eyes. "Seems your precious allies have abandoned you in your hour of need. How utterly... pathetic." Belail jeers.

The third villain chuckles darkly, cracking his knuckles with relish. "Perhaps you thought you could best us with their help, but it seems they've deserted you. No heroes to save the day today, my dear." Beezulbub mocked.

But despite their mocking words, the heroines stand tall, Their spirits unbroken, their resolve unyielding, for they know that true strength lies not in numbers or allies but in the courage to face adversity head-on, and by The spirit of The Lord of Hosts, even in the darkest of times.

"Brothers of darkness," one of the warrior angels intones, Jophiels' voice like a melody of steel and silk, "we have faced your kind before and emerged victorious. The people of this sacred place shall not fall under your wicked dominion."

Her companion Costello, equally resolute, adds, "By the grace of God, we stand as guardians of the innocent, defenders of the righteous. Your reign of terror ends here and now."

Costello and Jophiel Switched to their Angelic forms as the Demon lords charged. Costello uses her powerful whirlwind attacks and the sword of heavenly light. At the same time, Jophiel used her powers of fire and ice on her dual-sided blade. As Bezzulbub summons a swarm of insects attacking Costello, she blows away the bug swarm with a whirlwind attack, knocking Beez back and slashing his brittle insect-like skin with her sword. Jophiel launches an ice attack at Belial and Back'tor, causing them to suffer from frostbite injuries. Then Jophiel blasts them with flames, setting them ablaze. Bak'tor shakes it off and smacks Jophiel with his Giant lava and iron Axe, bruising her, and knocking her into a daze.

Belial now regaining his stance takes his giant lava and steel hammer and knocks Costello over the head knocking her out Jophiel gives one more swing at belial piercing his arm as she faints.

With a thunderous clash of steel against infernal might, the battle is joined, the fate of the church and its people hanging in the balance as light and darkness collide in a dance of eternal struggle.

As the echoes of battle fade, the once-serene atmosphere within the church is shattered by the ominous sound of heavy footsteps echoing in the nave. Through the splintered doors, a dark tide of eclipse forces spills into the sacred sanctuary, their sinister presence casting long shadows across the hallowed ground.

With their victory over the defenders now assured, the malevolent figures advance with predatory grace, their eyes gleaming with malice as they survey the trembling congregation before them.

Panicked whispers fill the air as the innocent worshippers huddle together, their fear palpable in the stifling darkness that envelops them. Mothers clutch their children tightly while the elderly seek refuge behind crumbling pillars, their frail hands trembling with trepidation.

But even as despair threatens to consume them, a flicker of defiance ignites within the hearts of the faithful, for they know that in the face of evil, hope can still shine bright, like a beacon in the night.

As the echoes of battle fade, the once-serene atmosphere within the church is shattered by the ominous sound of heavy footsteps echoing in the nave. Through the splintered doors, a dark tide of eclipse forces spills into the sacred sanctuary, their sinister presence casting long shadows across the hallowed ground.

And so, as the eclipse forces close in, ready to seize their helpless prey, the people of the church stand united in silent resistance, their unwavering faith a shield against the encroaching darkness.

As it is written, Do not be afraid of what you are about to suffer. I tell you, the devil will put some of you in prison to test you, and you will suffer persecution for ten days. Be faithful, even to the point of death, and I will give you the crown of life. (Revelation 2:10))

Eclipse gathered thousands of God's people as prisoners of war. They bound the hands of the saints and covered their eyes. They pushed around and brutalized the saints of the highest God. They killed the wounded in the church with no mercy. They marched innocent Men, Women, and children of various ages out of the city . North toward the coven and the Frost Peak fortress. The prisoners said prayers under their breath to gain strength to endure just as Jesus and countless other saints were persecuted for their righteous testimony and faith in God. Hundreds of miles later, they reach a massive castle-like prison complex west of the Coven. The Demons celebrated their victory of revenge by roaring, jeering, drinking, and snarling wickedly. When unbeknownst to them, Costello and Jophiel woke up knocked out of their angelic heroine form. Costello: "Jophiel, do you feel that? The energy of malevolence thickens the air. Our foes celebrate prematurely, unaware that their victory is but a fleeting illusion."

Jophiel: "Indeed, Costello. Though we were felled in battle, our spirits remain unbroken. Let them revel in their moment of triumph, for it shall be short-lived."

Costello: "Their arrogance blinds them to the resilience of the celestial realm. We may have been knocked down, but we rise stronger with each passing moment. The tide of battle shall soon turn in our favor."

Jophiel: "Let us bide our time, sister, and gather our strength in the shadows. When the moment is ripe, we shall emerge from the depths of defeat to vanquish our foes with righteous fury."

Costello: "For even in the darkest hour, the light of justice shall prevail. Our enemies may celebrate now, but they shall soon learn the folly of underestimating the might of Costello and Jophiel, warrior angels of the divine."

Jophiel and Costello looked at the church in shock as they took them prisoners. They burned with righteous anger and regret. "This is all our fault if we had just.." "No, this is their fault. Don't put that on us like Micheal said. We can't save everybody. We do what we can," Jophiel reminded Costello. "You, right," Costello added. The two flew up in a snap to give their commander a situation report. "How are things? "Mike says as he slays another fallen angel lackey. "It's Bad Bak' tor, Belial, and Beezulbub have destroyed the capital, ran the people to another city, and taken the church as prisoners of war. The Eclipse forces have killed thousands of soldiers and civilians, sir."Costello Reported! These words crushed Micheal. The hero angelic commander listens in grave silence as the report of the demons' major victory on Earth reaches his ears. A heavyweight settles upon his shoulders, the burden of responsibility pressing down upon him like a mountain.

His heart aches with the knowledge that his troops have suffered defeat, their valiant efforts thwarted by the forces of darkness. Doubt gnaws at his resolve, whispering insidious accusations of failure and inadequacy.

But even as despair threatens to overwhelm him, the commander knows that he cannot afford to dwell on his feelings of guilt and remorse. The fate of Earth hangs in the balance, and he alone bears the responsibility of defending it against the encroaching threat of the demons.

With a heavy heart and a mind torn by indecision, the commander weighs his options. Should he abandon his mission to pursue a smaller threat, risking the unleashing of a greater calamity upon the unsuspecting inhabitants of Earth? Or should he stay the course, holding fast against the relentless tide of darkness, even as his own doubts threaten to consume him?

In the end, duty calls him to action. With a steely resolve born of necessity, the commander sets aside his personal anguish and reaffirms his commitment to the greater good. For he knows that in the face of overwhelming darkness, even the smallest flicker of light can illuminate the path to victory.

"Warrior sisters heed my command," the angelic commander's voice resonates with unwavering resolve, cutting through the tension like a clarion call. "The victory of darkness may anger us, but we shall not be swayed by our emotions nor distracted by how we think things should be."

His eyes blaze with determination as he continues, "This is our mission, bestowed upon us by the Lord of hosts himself. And though the forces of darkness may seem insurmountable, remember that it is not by power, but by the spirit of our divine purpose that we shall emerge victorious."

He clasps their shoulders with a firm grip, imparting strength and reassurance. "Go forth, my brave sisters, with faith as your shield and righteousness as your sword. Together, let us stand against the tide of darkness, for we are warriors of the light, and no shadow can withstand the radiance of our resolve." Micheal ordered resolutely his all the heveanly arch-Angels heard their commanders words and were incouraged.

Costello and Jophiel Swiftly flew back to The Horde ready to throw down.

CHAPTER 6

Unbroken

Weeping may be for a night, but joy comes in the morning - Psalms 30:5

Seven Days had passed since the church assault. On the 8th day, Costello and Jophiel began to sing to The lord on the ruins of the church. They sang in an unknown heavenly tongue inviting the power of the holy spirit to strengthen. Then Blue and purple flames descended, bathed in light swirling like a pillar of fire on the two angelic heroines strengthening their powers. The holy spirit also gave them more wisdom and incite to beat the enemy. The Angels had learned their mistake. They were so busy trying to fight and overthinking that they almost forgot. The God they serve is Jehovah Gibbor, The Lord strong and mighty, The Lord mighty in battle with him, nothing is impossible. The Demons were patrolling the capital, non the wiser of what was about to happen. Jophiel approached the demons, asking, "Where's Bak'tor? We have unfinished Business". "You'll regret coming back, Jophiel"! Demon jeered Bak'tor. Jophiel, radiant in her celestial beauty and clad in shimmering purple tights and silver armor, steps onto the battlefield, her black kinky Afro framing her determined countenance. Her wings, one ablaze with fiery fury and the other shimmering with icy resolve unfurl majestically behind her, a testament to her dual nature.

With her sword, forged from the elements of fire and ice, gripped firmly in hand, she advances to meet her adversary, Bak'tar, the formidable bull humanoid clad in thick, spiky armor and wielding a lava axe with deadly precision.

Their clash sends shockwaves rippling through the air, the clash of fire against ice, of strength against agility, echoing across the battlefield. Each strike is met with a counterstrike, a dance of blades and powers that seems to defy the very laws of nature.

Jophiel's determination burns bright, her movements fluid and graceful as she harnesses the power of both fire and ice to outmaneuver her opponent. Bak'tar, for his part, roars with primal fury, his axe swinging with brute force as he seeks to overwhelm his ethereal foe.

But Jophiel is undaunted, her resolve unyielding as she presses forward, channeling the elemental forces at her command into a devastating onslaught. With a final, decisive blow, she shatters

BAK'TAR

Bak'tar's defenses, sending him crashing to the ground in defeat.

As the dust settles and the battlefield grows quiet, Jophiel stands victorious, her sword held aloft in triumph. For in the eternal struggle between light and darkness, she is a beacon of hope, a warrior of the divine, and her courage knows no bounds.

Costello finds Bezzulbub off guard. As Costello, the radiant heroine with flowing blonde locks and majestic white feathered wings, dons her gleaming armor adorned with gold and ivory accents, she clutches her sword of heavenly light bestowed upon her by the divine. With a resolute gaze, she sets forth to seek vengeance upon her formidable adversary, Beelzebub, the sinister lord of the flies.

Upon reaching the battleground, Costello braces herself for the impending confrontation, her heart filled with righteous fury and determination. With a flick of her wrist, she commands the winds to swirl around her, their gentle whispers echoing her resolve to triumph over evil.

Beelzebub, the insect humanoid with malevolent eyes and a swarm of deadly insects at his command, sneers at Costello's approach, his twisted grin belying the malice within. With a wave of his hand, he summons forth his legion of buzzing minions, their wings humming with anticipation of battle.

Undaunted by the swarm of insects that darken the sky, Costello raises her sword aloft, its ethereal light piercing through the darkness with divine radiance. With a mighty sweep, she unleashes a tempest of wind, her powers amplifying the force of her strikes as she cuts through the swarm with precision and grace.

The air crackles with energy as Costello and Beelzebub engage in a fierce battle of wills, the clash of their powers resonating with the intensity of a storm. With each stroke of her sword and every gust of wind she commands, Costello chips away at her adversary's defenses, her determination unwavering in the face of darkness.

In a final, decisive blow, Costello harnesses the full force of her elemental powers, unleashing a cyclone of wind that engulfs Beelzebub in a whirlwind of divine wrath. With a triumphant cry, she watches as her foe is vanquished, his form dissipating into the ether as the winds of justice carry his malevolence away.

With her revenge exacted and her honor restored, Costello lowers her sword; her wings spread wide in victory. Though the battle may be won, she knows that her duty as a defender of the light is endless, and she stands ever-vigilant against the forces of darkness that threaten the world she holds dear. Jophiel, adorned in her regal purple tights and silver armor, strides forward with determination, her black kinky Afro framing her resolute features. At her side stands her sister-in-arms, Costello, a vision of angelic beauty with her golden and white armor gleaming in the light, her pure white feathered wings outstretched. Together, they are a formidable force, ready to face their adversary once more.

BELIAL

Their opponent, Belial, the sinister lizard humanoid with wicked red eyes, stands before them, clad in spiked armor plates and wielding a molten bronze hammer with deadly intent. His menacing presence fills the air with tension as he prepares to unleash his wrath upon the angelic warriors.

But Jophiel and Costello are undaunted, their spirits unyielding as they prepare to face their foe once more. With a nod of silent understanding, they advance, their weapons at the ready, their powers swirling around them like a tempest.

Jophiel's sword, half ice, and half fire, crackles with elemental energy as she charges forward, while Costello's sword of divine light gleams with the radiance of God's power. Together, they unleash a torrent of attacks, their movements synchronized in perfect harmony as they strive to overcome their formidable adversary.

Belial, however, proves to be a relentless opponent, his molten hammer striking with ferocious strength as he seeks to crush his angelic foes. But Jophiel and Costello fight with unwavering resolve, their bond as sisters-in-arms strengthening their resolve with each passing moment.

With a final, concerted effort, they unleash a barrage of elemental and divine power, overwhelming Belial and sending him crashing to the ground in defeat. As the dust settles and the echoes of battle fade, Jophiel and Costello stand victorious, their sisterly bond unbroken and their faith in the light of God shining bright.

Captain Wells and his 4 four men one woman elite squad, cut off from communication in a bombed building, initiated a plan President Black approved before the war. A daring stealth mission into Willowbrook Hollows Eclispse base in the forest. The mission is to infiltrate undetected stealth choppers, kill 7 Eclipse Commanders, and plant explosives on enemy equipment, destroying as much as possible. Then, exfiltrate back to Sancturia alive. Captain Wells addressed his elite team of special operations forces, their faces obscured by the darkness of the night, their resolve unwavering despite the gravity of their mission.

"Listen up, team," he began, his voice low and commanding. "Our objective is clear: vengeance for the lives lost and the capital destroyed. We've been tasked by the President to infiltrate the enemy headquarters, eliminate their top commanders, and extract alive."

His gaze swept over his team, each member poised and ready for action, their weapons gleaming in the moonlight.

"We'll approach under the cover of darkness, utilizing the latest in stealth technology and night vision equipment. Our stealth helicopters will get us in close, but from there, it's up to us to move swiftly and silently."

He paused, his expression steely with determination.

BEELZEBUB

"Weapons hot, eyes sharp. Our enemies won't know what hit them. Let's give them the payback they deserve and make every shot count. Move out."

As Captain Wells and his team approached the massive eclipse headquarters, they moved with calculated precision, their mission clear in their minds. Two of their team members positioned themselves as snipers, their rifles trained on the seven commanders, ready to eliminate them with deadly accuracy.

With a series of silent shots, the commanders fell, their demise unnoticed amidst the chaos that ensued. Meanwhile, the rest of the team infiltrated the base, swiftly dispatching enemies as they moved through the shadows, planting explosives strategically to ensure the destruction of the enemy stronghold.

But as they prepared to detonate the charges and make their escape, they were confronted by an unexpected adversary—a mythical demonic elf princess named Jezebel. With her beautiful yet menacing presence, she wielded two mini axes coated in toxic slime, her magical powers, and elf demons at her command.

Despite their training and firepower, Captain Wells and his team found themselves overwhelmed by Jezebel's onslaught. Her attacks were swift and relentless, her toxic slime causing havoc among their ranks. In a desperate bid for survival, they fought with all their might, but it seemed as though they were facing insurmountable odds.

In their darkest moment, however, divine intervention came to their aid. Unbeknownst to them, an angel had prayed for their protection, and God answered their prayers. With supernatural strength and resilience, they managed to escape the clutches of Jezebel and her forces, their lives spared by a higher power.

As they regrouped and made their retreat, Captain Wells and his team knew that they had narrowly escaped death, their faith in their mission and each other stronger than ever. And though the battle had been fierce, they were determined to continue their fight against the forces of darkness, knowing that they had been granted a second chance by the grace of God.

Captain Wells detonated the C-40 explosives his planted in the base before they escaped. Ka-Boom hundred of explosions one after another creates a bright fire ball lighting up the darkness of the forest. With the mission complete the slowly walked away like a action movie hero.

An angel named Esther comes to the rescue, sitting in the cut.

As Esther, the angelic heroine, faced off against Jezebel, the demonic elf princess, their contrasting appearances mirrored the battle between light and darkness.

Esther, her long silky black hair flowing behind her, her yellow skin radiant beneath the glow of her red flaming wings, wielded her new red and gold guan dao with grace and precision. Her Chinese-style golden and red armor gleamed in the light, a testament to her divine heritage.

Jezebel, with her horns and greenish skin, exuded an otherworldly beauty that belied the darkness within. Clad in a green dress and wielding two green mini axes dripping with toxic green slime, she moved with a feline grace that spoke of her deadly prowess.

As they circled each other, Esther spoke with a voice filled with determination. "Jezebel, your reign of darkness ends here. I will not let your love for plants be twisted into a tool for evil."

STEALTH CHOPPER FLYING BETWEEN MOUNTAINS

Jezebel laughed, the sound tinged with malice. "Oh, sweet Esther, you underestimate the power of nature. Plants are not mere tools—they are allies, and they will aid me in my quest for domination."

With a flick of her wrist, Jezebel unleashed a barrage of toxic slime toward Esther, who countered with a blast of red fire from her hands, creating a blazing barrier between them.

"Nature may be powerful, but the light of righteousness will always prevail," Esther declared, her eyes flashing with determination as she summoned a whirlwind of fire to engulf Jezebel.

The battle raged on, the clash of fire and slime echoing through the air as two powerful forces collided. But in the end, it was Esther's unwavering faith and righteous fury that emerged victorious, banishing Jezebel back into the darkness of the forest from whence she came.

In the darkness of a military prison camp, far removed from the world's gaze, a silent suffering unfolds—a harrowing tale of Christians held captive by an evil, demonic army, their only crime their unwavering belief in God and his righteousness.

Within the confines of their prison cells, these brave souls endure unimaginable hardships, their faith tested with each passing day. Stripped of their freedom and dignity, they are subjected to cruel and inhumane treatment at the hands of their captors, who seek to crush their spirits and extinguish the light of their faith.

But even in the face of such adversity, the prisoners refuse to surrender their beliefs. They gather in secret, their voices raised in prayer and song, finding solace and strength in their shared faith. Despite the constant threat of punishment, they cling to hope, knowing that they are not alone in their suffering.

Meanwhile, outside the walls of the prison camp, the world remains largely unaware of the plight of these persecuted Christians. Their stories go untold, their suffering hidden from view, as the evil forces that hold them captive continue to perpetrate their atrocities with impunity.

But even in the darkness of their captivity, a flicker of light remains—a beacon of hope that refuses to be extinguished. For these brave souls know that they are not forgotten, that their faith will sustain them through the darkest of nights, and that one day, justice will prevail, and they will be free once more. Lilith went to Dark Lord Malphas to inform him of his HQ being destroyed. " I have some bad news for you: your bases were destroyed, and many of your commanders and soldiers are dead at the HQ. A team of elite soldiers went in and eliminated many of your troops and officers, planted explosives, and blew up your base; Jezebel tried to stop them but was unsuccessful. I've been lying low, knowing that these angels are coming after us. Their God emboldens them, and I saw this in the crystal ball I used to monitor what's going on,". Lilith reported. "ah roar," Lord Darkbane raged with perfect hate and anger, pondering what to do. "I know well. Start executing these God lovers one by one until Sentinel and the angels cease operations. Lilith Star

ARCH-ANGEL ESTHER

bringing a group of prisoners into the arena in your coven to be executed," " Dark Bane ordered, "ok, will do, but if you cause the angels to come after me, I'll make you pay." Lilith cautioned Lord Malphas. Day by day, for ten days, prisoners were executed in public executions to shake their faith, but God had already warned them that some would be killed for his name's sake. They knew each tragedy was a win on the other side. They wavered not and waited on the deliverance of God. They cried out to the Lord, "How long, oh lord, till you send a redeemer to free us and avenge our blood"? The church cried out. "Hold on a little while longer until the number of you who are to be martyred is completed." The lord replied. Jophiel was ordered by Micheal to free the prisoners, and she didn't know how she knew God would provide. She entered the jail, setting off an alarm in human form. The guards quickly arrest her. Jophiel resists the entire way to her cell block. The guards grew tired of the struggle and threw her on the ground and beat her. Jophiel was tired of evil, so she punched two guards and threw a third guard across the cell block. She walked to her cell to rest. The guards were scared of her fighting ability; nobody had ever put up that much resistance before. As Costello, the courageous heroine, sneaks a human into the execution lines under the guise of her human form, she waits in the shadows, her heart heavy with the weight of the impending danger. As the moment of execution arrives, she begins to sing a hymn of praise to God, her voice pure and unwavering, filling the air with divine grace. In a flash of golden light, she transforms into her angelic form, clad in golden and white armor, wielding a sword of light and boasting pure white feathered wings that glisten in the sunlight.

With swift and decisive strikes, Costello dispatches the guards with righteous fury, her sword of light slicing through their evil defenses as if they were made of nothing but air. With a powerful swing, she cleaves a hole into the arena, freeing the captives and leading them to safety.

But her victory is short-lived, as Lilith, the supreme witch, and fallen angel, reveals her true form, her pink and green flaming wings a stark reminder of her twisted nature. With deceptive charm and deadly power, Lilith attacks Costello, her flames searing the air with malevolence. The supreme witch and wizard, their faces twisted with malice and contempt, stand before the angelic heroine, their voices dripping with disdain.

"Costello," the supreme witch Lilith sneers, her pink and green flaming wings casting an eerie glow around her, "you dare to interfere with our twisted execution game? You think you can defy us and escape unscathed?"

The wizard, his eyes gleaming with dark intent beneath his wizard robe and hat, adds with a malevolent chuckle, "Your actions reek of arrogance, angel. You may have saved these people for now, but mark my words. Your interference will not go unpunished."

SOPHIA ARCH-ANGEL

Together, their powers combine in a sinister display of dark magic, and they confront Costello with a chilling warning.

"We will not rest until we have exacted our vengeance upon you and all who stand with you," Lilith declares, her voice echoing with ominous finality. "You may have won this battle, but the war is far from over. And when the time comes, you will rue the day you dared to defy us."

With a wicked laugh, the supreme witch and wizard vanish into the shadows, leaving Costello to ponder the ominous threat that hangs over her like a dark cloud. But even in the face of such malevolence, she remains undaunted, her faith unwavering as she prepares to face whatever challenges lie ahead.

Undeterred, Costello faces her adversary with courage and determination, knowing that her main priority is the safety of the people she has sworn to protect. She fends off Lilith's attacks with skillful precision, her focus unwavering even as the evil wizard joins the fray in his sinister robe and hat.

With a final, decisive blow, Costello incapacitates her foes, knowing that judgment will come from a higher power. Leading the brave saints down the mountain towards the desert underground base, she assures them of their safety, her voice filled with compassion and strength.

"We may have faced darkness today, but we shall not be consumed by it," she declares, her words echoing through the underground tunnels. "Together, we shall find refuge and strength in the light of righteousness. For even in the depths of despair, there is hope, and in the face of evil, there is courage. Let us press on, for our journey is not yet over."

After the fiasco in the Coven arena, Jophiel knows it's time for her to take action.

As Jophiel, disguised in human form, begins to encourage the prisoners of war with songs of hope and faith, her voice rises above the din of their suffering, filling the prison with a sense of divine presence. Holding church services amidst the dire and inhumane circumstances, she offers a beacon of light in the darkness, helping the prisoners to hold onto their faith in the face of brutalization by ruthless and wicked soldiers.

As she sings songs of deliverance and hope, the power of God fills the prison, empowering Jophiel's angelic abilities of fire and ice. Her sword, forged with half fire and half ice, gleams with righteous fury, her purple heroic tights and shining silver armor reflecting the divine light that surrounds her. Her beautiful kinky black fro and brown skin radiate with the purity of her intentions.

With swift and decisive strikes, Jophiel slays the sadistic guards who have inflicted untold suffering upon the prisoners. Her powers of fire and ice blaze and freeze with divine authority, cutting through the walls of the prison-like a hot knife through butter. With each swing of her sword, she creates a path to freedom, leading thousands of prisoners toward the desert and safety.

THE MOUNTAIN TOP PRISON

As they emerge into the open air, the prisoners look upon Jophiel with awe and gratitude, their faces illuminated by the light of liberation. For in their darkest hour, she has been their savior, their guardian angel, leading them out of the depths of despair and into the promise of a new dawn. And though the journey ahead may be fraught with challenges, they walk with renewed hope, knowing that they are not alone, for the hand of God guides them every step of the way. Jophiel rendezvous with Costello and the other saints in the desert.

As Jophiel, disguised in human form, begins to encourage the prisoners of war with songs of hope and faith, her voice rises above the din of their suffering, filling the prison with a sense of divine presence. Holding church services amidst the dire and inhumane circumstances, she offers a beacon of light in the darkness, helping the prisoners to hold onto their faith in the face of brutalization by ruthless and wicked soldiers.

As she sings songs of deliverance and hope, the power of God fills the prison, empowering Jophiel's angelic abilities of fire and ice. Her sword, forged with half fire and half ice, gleams with righteous fury, her purple heroic tights and shining silver armor reflecting the divine light that surrounds her. Her beautiful kinky black fro and brown skin radiate with the purity of her intentions.

With swift and decisive strikes, Jophiel slays the sadistic guards who have inflicted untold suffering upon the prisoners. Her powers of fire and ice blaze and freeze with divine authority, cutting through the walls of the prison-like a hot knife through butter. With each swing of her sword, she creates a path to freedom, leading thousands of prisoners toward the desert and safety.

As they emerge into the open air, the prisoners look upon Jophiel with awe and gratitude, their faces illuminated by the light of liberation. For in their darkest hour, she has been their savior, their guardian angel, leading them out of the depths of despair and into the promise of a new dawn. And though the journey ahead may be fraught with challenges, they walk with renewed hope, knowing that they are not alone, for the hand of God guides them every step of the way.

As Costello, the angelic heroine, looks upon the people with compassion, her heart heavy with the weight of their suffering, she raises her voice in a prayer of healing and blessing.

"May the light of God shine upon you," she sings, her voice pure and filled with divine grace. "May his mercy and love envelop you, washing away the pain and sorrow that burden your hearts."

With each word of her prayer, bright lights descend from above, bathing the people in their radiant glow. The healing power of the virtue angels of God flows through the crowd, touching each individual with a gentle hand, soothing their injuries, and wiping away their tears.

Miracles unfold before their eyes as wounds close and broken spirits are lifted, replaced with a newfound sense of hope and peace. The people raise their voices in praise, their gratitude overflowing as they witness the hand of God at work in their lives.

For in this moment, justice is served, and the evil that sought to bring them harm is thwarted by the power of divine intervention. Costello, the angelic heroine, bows her head in reverence, knowing that she is but an instrument of God's will, a vessel through which his love and compassion may flow.

As the people rejoice in their newfound freedom and healing, they lift their voices in praise to the name of God, grateful for the angels who have come to their aid in their hour of need. For truly, the Lord is just and his judgments righteous, and his mercy endures forever.

As Jophiel and Costello lead the newly renewed Saints through the unforgiving desert, a large group of eclipse forces suddenly blocks their path, their menacing presence casting a shadow over the weary travelers. With weapons drawn and malice in their eyes, the enemy soldiers move to surround the Saints, intent on finishing them off for daring to escape.

But just as the tension reaches its peak, something miraculous happens. The commander of the division, moved by an unexplained sense of mercy, raises his hand and commands his soldiers to stand down. "Don't fire," he orders, his voice filled with unexpected compassion.

However, one soldier, driven by fear or defiance, disobeys this order and raises his weapon. Before anyone can react, a bolt of lightning streaks down from the heavens, striking the soldier down in an instant. The others, witnessing the divine punishment before their very eyes, scatter and flee in terror, their hearts gripped with fear of the wrath of the Lord of the Heavenly Hosts.

In the aftermath of this miraculous intervention, Jophiel and Costello continue to lead the Saints through the desert, their faith unwavering in the face of adversity. With each step, they draw closer to the stronghold where Sentinel troops await, ready to provide medical treatment and refuge.

But as they arrive, they are met with a sight beyond their expectations. God has intervened once again, and the refugees are not only safe but miraculously healed of their injuries and ailments. The stronghold is filled with a sense of awe and wonder as the Saints bear witness to the power of divine intervention, their hearts overflowing with gratitude and praise.

And so, under the watchful gaze of Jophiel and Costello, the Saints find sanctuary in the strong-sands stronghold, their bodies healed and their spirits renewed, thanks to the boundless mercy and grace of the Lord. Jophiel and Costello congratulated each other on the epic victory when they trusted God to move, and he did.

Jophiel: "Costello, what a miraculous rescue that was! To see thousands of prisoners of war freed from their captivity and healed of their injuries—it fills my heart with gratitude."

Costello: "Indeed, Jophiel. It was a testament to the power of divine intervention and the unwavering faith of those we rescued. To witness their liberation and healing firsthand was truly awe-inspiring."

Jophiel: "I couldn't agree more. And to think, it all started with a simple act of compassion and courage. Your bravery in leading the charge and my intervention with the power of God—it was a perfect combination."

Costello: "It was an honor to fight alongside you, Jophiel. Your strength and determination inspired us all. And to see the faces of those we rescued, filled with hope and gratitude, it reaffirms why we fight against the forces of darkness."

Jophiel: "Our mission is far from over, Costello. But with the faith and courage of those we've rescued and the power of God guiding our steps, I have no doubt that we will continue to make a difference in the world."

Costello: "Yes, Jophiel. As long as there are those in need of rescue and redemption, we will be there to answer the call. Together, we will shine as beacons of light in the darkness, bringing hope and healing wherever we go."

Jophiel: "Indeed, Costello. Together, we are unstoppable."

Back in Sanctuaria, Presidents Blackwell and Morgan order

General Stormheart spent little time executing the orders of Presidents Blackwell and Morgan. With precision and efficiency, he mobilized a massive defensive perimeter in the new city, integrating it seamlessly with the network of defenses across the nation.

Every weapon at their disposal was brought to bear, from the awe-inspiring light-beam weapon of God that repelled demons to the cutting-edge prototypes of robotic angels and flamethrowers armed with heavenly fire. Artillery shells, attack helicopters, Shadow blaster A5 Sentinel Tanks, naval battle groups, drones, eight-gen stealth fighter jets, hypersonic/ Petra-sonic missiles .jet aircraft, advanced lasers, Sky Sentry 800 air defenses, top-tier sig spear rifles, anti-tank/ anti-air rocket launchers, MLRS 4.0, and advanced space guardian coverage were all deployed in strategic locations throughout the defensive perimeter.

Ground forces numbering in the thousands, tens of thousands, and even hundreds of thousands were stationed in a layered defense strategy, ready to repel any enemy incursion with unwavering resolve. General Stormheart ensured that every soldier was equipped and trained to the highest standard, ready to face whatever threat may come their way. Equipped with billions of rounds of armor-piercing explosive ammunition

As the defensive perimeter took shape, General Stormheart stood at its heart, a beacon of strength and determination. With the full force of their nation's military might behind them, they were prepared to defend their city and their people at all costs. Any enemy that dared to cross their path would be met with swift and decisive action, vanquished by the unwavering resolve of those who stood in their defense.

They also armed the civilians who weren't already armed.

Esther, the anglic heroine, clad in her resplendent gold and red armor. Stands the amidst the tranquil beauty of the forest. She raises her guan dao and continues playing a heavenly melody

Demon Python: "What is this wretched noise? It grates on my ears like nails on a chalkboard!"

Esther: "It seems my music disturbs the peace of demons. Perhaps it is a reminder of the harmony they have forsaken."

Demon Python: "Silence, angel! Your music will not save you from my wrath!"

As Esther continues to play, she is suddenly interrupted by a sinister hiss behind her. Turning, she sees a massive green viper, its frills flared, and venomous fangs bared.

Esther: "Ah, it seems I have an unwelcome visitor."

Demon Python: "Esther, you meddlesome angel! You think you can beat my sister, Jezebel, and escape my vengeance?"

Esther: "I defeated Jezebel with the power of righteousness, Python. And I will do the same to you if necessary."

Demon Python: "You may have bested my sister, but you will not defeat me!"

With a roar of rage, the demon python lunges forward, its massive form moving with surprising speed. Esther dodges the attack, her guandao flashing as she strikes back with precision and grace.

Esther: "Your sister's defeat was her own doing, Python. Do not make the same mistake."

Demon Python: "I will not be so easily defeated, angel! I command the forces of darkness!"

As the demon python summons forth legions of snakes to aid him, Esther finds herself surrounded by a writhing mass of serpents. Undeterred, she fights on, her guandao slicing through the snakes with ease.

Esther: "Your minions cannot save you, Python. Face me with your own strength!"

Demon Python: "You may have vanquished my snakes, but you cannot withstand my venom!"

With a final, desperate lunge, the demon python strikes at Esther with its venomous fangs. But Esther is ready, her guandao striking true and piercing the demon python's heart.

Esther: "It is finished, Python. Now, Skirm away like the defeated foe you are."

As the demon python slithers away, defeated, Esther takes a moment to catch her breath, the forest around her silent once more. Though the battle was long and arduous, she emerged victorious, her faith and courage unwavering in the face of darkness.

CHAPTER 7

Into the Darkness of Void

The light shines in the darkness, and the darkness has not overcome it - John 1:5

He uncovers the deep out of darkness and brings deep darkness to light. -Job 12:22

Though you soar aloft like the eagle, though your nest is set among the stars, from there I will bring you down, declares the LORD. -Obadiah 1:4

Who made the Bear and Orion, the Pleiades and the chambers of the south;

Job 9:9

And I will show wonders in the heavens above and signs on the earth below, blood, and fire, and vapor of smoke; the sun shall be turned to darkness and the moon to blood, before the day of the Lord comes, the great and magnificent day. - Acts 2:19-20

Then I heard the number of those who were sealed: 144,000 from all the tribes of Israel.

Revelation 7:8

...And I will appoint my two witnesses, and they will prophesy for 1,260 days, clothed in sackcloth." They are "the two olive trees" and the two lampstands, and "they stand before the Lord of the earth." If

anyone tries to harm them, fire comes from their mouths and devours their enemies. This is how anyone who wants to harm them must die. They have the power to shut up the heavens so that it will not rain during the time they are prophesying, and they have the power to turn the waters into blood and strike the earth with every kind of plague as often as they want.

-Revelation 11:3-6

THE ETERNAL PROPHETS CALLING DOWN FIRE FROM HEAVEN

The multiple victories of the Forces of Heaven and Avalaria severely weakened and struck back the wicked, crushing darkness with light. Eclipse forces halted their offensive to recover and reconstitute. As the battered and wounded leaders of the Eclipse force staggered back to the safety of Willow Brook Forest, their

resolve remained unbroken. Malaphas, his dark aura flickering with defiance, convened an urgent council among his generals. As Jezebel and Python, both nursing their wounds surveyed the troops, their frustration simmered beneath the surface like molten lava.

"Pathetic!" Jezebel spat, her voice dripping with disdain. "Is this the best you can muster? We bleed for this cause, and yet you cower like frightened children!"

Python, his gaze piercing through the ranks, echoed her sentiment with a snarl. "You call yourselves soldiers of the Eclipse? I've seen newborn demons with more spine than you lot!"

The troops shifted uncomfortably, their eyes avoiding the fiery glares of their wounded leaders.

"We expect better from you," Jezebel continued, her voice a whip crack in the air. "If you wish to survive this war, you will fight like demons possessed!"

Python's fists clenched, his anger palpable. "You will not disgrace us again," he growled. "Or you'll answer to me personally."

With the weight of their commanders' disappointment hanging heavy in the air, the troops knew that failure was not an option. They would either rise to the occasion or face the wrath of Jezebel and Python, wounded but still formidable in their fury. Beezulbub, nursing his injuries with a scowl etched upon his face, limped forward with a venomous glare directed at Bak'tor and Dark Lord Malphas.

"Look at me!" he bellowed, his voice a thunderous echo in the forest. "I am Beelzebub, and I will not be treated like some insignificant imp! These wounds are a disgrace, a stain upon my honor!"

Bak'tor, taken aback by the outburst, bristled with anger. "Mind your tongue, Beelzebub," he growled, his own injuries forgotten in the heat of the moment. "We are all suffering in this war, not just you."

But Beelzebub's fury knew no bounds as he rounded on Dark Lord Malphas, his eyes ablaze with righteous indignation. "And you, Malphas!" he seethed. "Your leadership has brought us nothing but misery and defeat! If you had half the wit of a gnat, perhaps we wouldn't be in this predicament!"

ARCH-ANGEL HANIEL

Dark Lord Malphas, his patience wearing thin, fixed Beelzebub with a cold, steely gaze. "Watch your words, Beelzebub," he warned his voice like ice. "Or I'll ensure your next wound is far more grievous than any you've suffered thus far."

With tensions simmering dangerously, the wounded leaders of the Eclipse force stood at the precipice of discord, their unity teetering on the edge of collapse. Only time would tell if their fractured alliance could withstand the weight of their anger and resentment.

"Brothers and sisters," Malaphas intoned, his voice resonating with power, "though we have suffered grievous losses, our spirits remain undimmed. We shall rise from the ashes of defeat, stronger and fiercer than ever before!"

Belial, his wounds still seeping with ichor, nodded in solemn agreement. "Our adversaries may have struck us down, but they have not broken our will," he declared. "With each blow they deliver, we shall only grow more determined to claim victory!"

Bak'tor, his eyes blazing with fury, slammed his fist against the ancient trees surrounding them. "Let us not dwell on our past defeats," he growled. "For we have tasted triumph before, and we shall taste it again! With Behemoth at our side, we shall crush the forces of Avaral beneath our heels!"

And so, with their ranks bolstered and their spirits renewed, the Eclipse force prepared to unleash their wrath upon the new capital of Avalaria. Little did the angelic forces know the darkness lurking within the depths of Willow Brook Forest was about to rise once more with a vengeance that would shake the very foundations of their world.

Lilith, her usually composed demeanor shattered, paced frantically within the confines of her sanctum, the flickering flames of her pink and green aura casting eerie shadows upon the walls.

"We've meddled too deeply in matters beyond our comprehension," she murmured, her voice laced with rare anxiety. "The spirit backlash... it speaks of judgment, of retribution for our sins against humanity and the Church."

The wizard, his own hands trembling with fear, nodded in grim agreement. "We've danced with darkness for too long," he whispered, his voice barely audible above the crackling of the arcane energies surrounding them. "And now, the consequences come knocking at our door."

Lilith's eyes blazed with a mixture of panic and determination as she turned to the demon lord standing before her, his presence a looming shadow in the dimly lit chamber.

"We have angered forces far beyond our comprehension," she warned, her voice trembling with reluctant resolve. "And they will not spare us in their wrath. Even our alliance with the Eclipse army and demonic forces may not shield us from the divine retribution that awaits."

Despite her reluctance, Lilith knew that her coven's fate was intertwined with the darkness they had embraced. And as much as she tried to keep them hidden in the shadows, the looming judgment of a higher power threatened to expose them all to the harsh light of divine justice.

As the two saints, imbued with divine power and accompanied by the multitude of refugees turned saints, approached the desert military research base, a sense of awe and reverence swept through the encampment. The refugees recognized these figures as the legendary Eternal prophets, risen from the dead with the authority of heaven itself.

FALLEN ANGEL ESHETH AND HER TWO FORMS

Whispers spread like wildfire among the gathered multitude as they realized the significance of the prophets' arrival. These were the chosen vessels of God, blessed with the ability to wield the elements and unleash the plagues of divine judgment upon the wicked.

With hearts full of faith and determination, the top 144,000 saints gathered around the prophets, eager to learn from their wisdom and channel the power of Jesus's name.

Together, they set out on a treacherous journey from the desert base to the Frost-Peak fortress, where the sorcerers of Baal and the forces of darkness awaited. With each step, their resolve strengthened, fueled by the righteous fury of God's avenging angels.

At the summit of the fortress, amidst swirling storms and crackling lightning, the prophets and the saints prepared to unleash the full force of heaven's wrath upon the sorcerers of Baal. It would be a battle of epic proportions, a clash of divine power against the forces of darkness, as they sought to prove once and for all that God reigns supreme.

As the Eternal prophets and the 144,000 sealed saints ascended the frosty peak, a monstrous figure emerged from the swirling snowdrifts - the Snow Beast Guardian, a fearsome creature of ice and malice. Its massive form loomed over the saints, its icy breath freezing the very air around them.

With a thunderous roar, the Snow Beast Guardian warned of their impending doom, its voice echoing across the mountainside. But the prophets and saints stood firm, their faith unshaken by the creature's menacing presence.

"In the name of the Holy Spirit, we command you to stand down!" one of the prophets declared, his voice ringing out with divine authority.

But the Snow Beast Guardian only snarled in response, unleashing a horde of snow demons to assail the saints. Undeterred, the prophets and saints called upon the power of Jesus's name, commanding the elements to their will.

With a clash of thunder and lightning, an epic battle erupted upon the frosty peak. The air crackled with energy as fire and ice collided, and the ground shook beneath the weight of the combatants' fury.

The prophets and saints fought with valor and determination, their hearts ablaze with the righteousness of their cause. With every prayer uttered and every command spoken in Jesus's name, they pushed back against the onslaught of darkness.

In the end, it was the power of faith and the guiding light of the Holy Spirit that prevailed. With a final cry of triumph, the prophets and saints banished the Snow Beast Guardian and its minions back into the depths of the frozen abyss.

As the accusations rang out from the two Eternal prophets, Lilith and the wizard trembled with fear, their hearts heavy with guilt for their role in the atrocities committed against the saints of the highest. "It is written, "Do not touch my anointed ones; do my prophets no harm (Psalms 105:15)." The Prophets shouted, But in their prideful defiance, they hurled obscenities back at the prophets "I don't care why you're here, Lilith and Orpheus replied, attempting to shift the blame onto the Eclipse and the demon lords.

SNOW BEAST GUARDIAN

But the prophets would not be swayed by their excuses. With righteous indignation, they proclaimed that their crimes against humanity could not be excused, regardless of who had coerced them into committing such heinous acts.

In a dramatic showdown reminiscent of the biblical account of the prophets of Baal, the prophets and the sorcerers clashed in a battle of divine power and dark magic. Lightning crackled across the sky as fire and ice collided in a cataclysmic display of supernatural warfare. The Eternal Prophets spawned whirlwinds of ice, volcanic eruptions, and earthquakes, deplaying the power of he who sent them.

But in the end, it was the power of God's judgment that prevailed. With a final, resounding cry, the two Eternal prophets called down fire from heaven to consume the wicked coven, leaving nothing but ash in their wake.

As the flames licked at their heels, the members of the coven scattered in a desperate attempt to escape the divine

And so, as the snow-covered mountain echoed with the sounds of their cries, the coven learned a harsh lesson in humility and repentance. For the God of Elijah had arisen in judgment against them, and none could stand against the power of his righteous fury.

As the echoes of battle faded and the snow-covered landscape fell silent once more, the prophets and saints stood victorious, a testament to the unwavering strength of their faith.

Lilith and Orpheus burned with anger as they got up from the snow. Knowing their coven had been once again destroyed, their faithful followers were now not emotionless and humbled by The Lord of Hosts. The sorcerers scattered across the snowy mountains, freezing and hurting from being scorched by heavenly fire, dazed and confused. "Don't worry, my children Bak'tor and Lord Malphas will pay for getting us involved in this mess. We'll dust off and head to the forest to arm ourselves. We will strike Eclipse and the demon army with guns and Majic," Lilith devously uttered. "They won't see it coming. I warned them, haha," She Laughed. The whole coven set out to do as Lilith commanded to take revenge. " I will assist you, my queen, in avenging the coven," Orpheus sounded resolute. "How noble of you, Orpheus," Lilith thanked

The Eternal Prophets and the saints teleported to Sanctaria. They Approached a hospital full of wounded and sick people. Compassion and the heart of The Lord moved them for the people. They ascended to the top of the hospital, lifted up their hands, and said, "By the God that created the heavens and the earth, these people shall be healed." At once, beautiful angels of virtue descended into the hospital, entered the rooms, and delivered

BEHEMOTH

healing to everyone, even the staff. The spirit of God filled the hospital as the sick arose and began dancing. Those close to death were now reinvigorated. The doctors recorded so many miracles science could not explain. It took 2 weeks to document them all. News of this glorious wonder spread, but God alone received the credit after all the Prophets were anointed to fulfill God's will, not their own. The Eternal Prophets were humble yet stoic and powerful as the scene transitions from the turmoil of Earth to the vast expanse of space, the celestial battlefield comes into view, a cosmic arena where the forces of light and darkness clash in a titanic struggle for supremacy. Archangels, including the fiery-haired hero Haniel, soar through the heavens amidst a swirling maelstrom of fallen angels, their flaming swords cutting through the darkness with righteous fury.

Despite the ongoing war on Earth, the archangels press forward, their determination unwavering as they draw closer to their ultimate objective. Haniel, with her blazing orange wings and twin flaming swords, radiates an aura of unmatched strength and courage, leading the celestial host toward her final showdown with the ancestral fallen angel demons.

Her destination Venus, where the fallen angel Esheth, Goddess of Sin, awaits their arrival. A formidable adversary, Esheth's metallic form glimmers with malevolent power, her steel sword poised for battle. But she is not without her own arsenal, capable of unleashing torrents of plasma from her hands and reshaping the very landscape with her control over the molten lava of the planet.

As Haniel approaches the planet, the heat of the sun causes her to sweat, which drips down her brow as the archangel breaches the atmosphere of Venus. The thick, reddish clouds in Venus's atmosphere are composed of carbon dioxide, nitrogen, and sulfur gas. The ratchet smell of burning super burns her nose, but she is resolute in her mission as her breath labors.

As Haniel confronted Esheth, Goddess of Sin, atop the fiery surface of Venus, their eyes locked in a fierce gaze, each one a reflection of the other's resolve and determination.

"Haniel, Archangel of the Most High," Esheth hissed, her voice dripping with malice. "You dare to challenge me, the rightful ruler of this domain? You and your kind have no place here!"

Haniel's response was firm and unwavering, her voice carrying the weight of divine authority. "Esheth, your reign of darkness ends now," she declared, her twin flaming swords held at the ready. "The light of righteousness will prevail, and your sins shall be judged."

Esheth scoffed, her metallic form shimmering with disdain. "You speak of righteousness, yet you serve a God who condemns without mercy," she retorted. "I embrace the darkness, for it is in darkness that true power lies."

But Haniel remained steadfast, her faith unshaken by Esheth's words of temptation. "Your power is nothing compared to the might of the Most High," she countered, her wings ablaze with divine fire. "In His name, I shall cast you down and bring an end to your tyranny."

With a roar of defiance, Esheth unleashed a torrent of plasma from her hands, the searing energy crackling through the air. But Haniel stood firm, her swords ablaze with righteous fury as she prepared to face her adversary in battle.

In the cosmic arena of Venus, amidst the swirling storms and fiery eruptions, the clash of light and darkness raged on. As the echoes of their confrontation reverberated through the heavens, only one truth remained certain: the outcome of this celestial duel would shape the fate of the cosmos for eternity.

The intensity of the battle reaches its peak. Blades clash, and energies collide as Haniel engages the forces of darkness in a cataclysmic struggle for the fate of the cosmos.

With each stroke of her flaming swords, Haniel presses forward, her resolve unyielding in the face of overwhelming opposition. As Esheth shifts and twists, her form morphing to meet the challenges posed by the archangel, Haniel remains steadfast, her faith in the righteousness of their cause unwavering.

In a climactic clash of titans, Haniel and Esheth meet in a whirlwind of fire and steel, their powers colliding in a dazzling display of celestial might. But in the end, it is the purity of Haniel's spirit and the strength of her conviction that proves victorious, as she delivers a final, decisive blow that vanquishes Esheth and brings an end to the reign of darkness.

As the dust settles and the echoes of battle fade into the void, Haniel stands triumphant, and her flaming wings outstretched against the backdrop of the cosmos. Though the war may continue to rage on, the victory won on Venus serves as a beacon of hope for all who fight in the name of light and righteousness. Indeed, the cosmic battles between the forces of light and darkness are far from over. As each confrontation unfolds, the stakes escalate to unimaginable heights, with the very fabric of the universe hanging in the balance.

With every clash of celestial titans, the intensity of the warfare reaches unprecedented levels, pushing the limits of both angelic and demonic power to their breaking points. From the depths of the cosmos to the furthest reaches of reality, the struggle between good and evil rages on with ferocity unmatched by any previous conflict.

Each battle serves as a crucible, testing the resolve and courage of those who fight for righteousness and justice. But as the forces of darkness continue to unleash their most fearsome weapons and tactics, the champions of light must rise to meet the challenge with unwavering determination and unwavering faith.

In the crucible of cosmic warfare, heroes are forged and legends are born. And as the heat of battle intensifies to over 9000°, only those who can withstand the searing flames of adversity will emerge victorious, securing the future of the universe for generations to come.

Esheth re-forms her liquid metallic body, injured but not defeated. "HA, You thought you could stop me. I'm headed to Earth by Tudalu Hannah. Nice try," Esheth glowed. She swiftly flies toward Earth, destruction on her mind. Haniel reports to Mike, "Micheal, we have a problem. I thought I beat Esheth, but she used her shapeshifting ability to escape, and shes barreling towards earth. I'm in pursuit. "Rodger, " Gabriel, Uriel, Raphael, and I are headed toward the asteroid belt for Baal, mercury the twins, pluto for Azrech, and Jupiter for Asmodeous. We're trying to wrap this operation up, but the regulars held us up significantly. Do what you can remember. Esther, Jophiel, and Costello are on earth. They could aid you," Micheal responded. "Rodger, I won't give in, I let you or God down," Haniel shouted out of breath.

CHAPTER 8

Whispers of Treachery

Praise the LORD, who is my rock.
He trains my hands for war
and gives my fingers skill for battle.
He is my loving ally and my fortress,
my tower of safety, my rescuer.
He is my shield, and I take refuge in him.
He makes the nations submit to me. - Psalm 144:1-2

Even closer to the sun near the planet Mercury dwells two wick Ancestral powers named Al'gid and Ral'gis. As Uriel, the mighty archangel, approached the scorching planet Mercury, the intensity of the heat threatened to engulf him. Yet, clad in armor of radiant gold and yellow flames, he pressed on with unwavering determination.

With his spear of yellow lightning and fire held aloft, Uriel radiated an aura of unmatched power and strength. His wings, ablaze with the brilliance of yellow flames, propelled him forward through the searing heat of the sun's closest companion.

As he descended upon the surface of Mercury, the very air crackled with the energy of his presence. With a command, he

called forth bolts of yellow lightning, their searing brilliance illuminating the harsh landscape below. And with a sweep of his spear, he unleashed torrents of yellow fire, scorching the ground with righteous fury.

Though the heat threatened to overwhelm him, Uriel remained resolute in his mission, for he knew that even amidst the inferno of battle, the light of righteousness would prevail. And as he stood upon the fiery surface of Mercury, he vowed to bring justice and victory to all who stood against the forces of darkness.

Mercury has a hot and cold side Al'gid on the hot side and Ral'gis on the cold side facing away from earth.As Uriel approached the fallen twins, their malevolent presence permeated the air, a sinister aura that filled the space with darkness and deceit. Ral'gis the blue-skinned twin, with sickly veins snaking across his skin, spoke first, his voice dripping with malice.

ARCH-ANGEL URIEL

"Well, well, well," he sneered, his eyes flashing with wicked delight. "Look what the cat dragged in. It seems we have a visitor, brother."

Al'gid, the red-skinned twin, his fiery horns ablaze with infernal energy, chuckled darkly. "Indeed we do, brother," he replied, his voice a sinister echo of his twin's. "And what brings the illustrious Archangel Uriel to our humble abode?"

Uriel's gaze remained steady, his spear of yellow lightning and fire poised for battle. "I have come to put an end to your reign of darkness," he declared, his voice resonating with divine authority. "Your deception and wickedness will no longer be tolerated."

The twins exchanged a knowing glance, their wicked smiles widening with amusement. "Oh, how quaint," the blue-skinned twin remarked, his tone dripping with sarcasm. "The mighty Archangel Uriel, here to play the hero."

The red-skinned twin chuckled darkly. "Tell us, Uriel," he taunted, his voice laced with malice. "Do you truly believe you can defeat us? We are the masters of deception, the lords of trickery. You are but a pawn in our game."

But Uriel remained undeterred, his resolve unwavering in the face of their taunts. With a steely gaze, he raised his spear high, ready to unleash the full force of his yellow lightning and fire against the fallen twins.

"For the light of righteousness shall always triumph over the darkness of deceit," Uriel proclaimed, his voice echoing through the shadows. "And today, your reign of wickedness comes to an end."

As the fallen twins launched their attack, Uriel stood firm, his spear of yellow lightning and fire ablaze with righteous fury. With a swift motion, he deflected their dark energy with a burst of his own, the clash of powers echoing through the celestial realm.

The blue-skinned twin conjured illusions, weaving a tapestry of deceit to confuse and disorient Uriel. But the archangel saw through the deception, his unwavering resolve guiding him through the shadows.

Meanwhile, the red-skinned twin unleashed torrents of fiery blasts, each one aimed with deadly precision. But Uriel's wings of yellow flames acted as a shield, deflecting the onslaught with ease.

With a mighty cry, Uriel retaliated, calling upon the power of his spear to unleash bolts of yellow lightning that crackled and danced across the battlefield. The fallen twins recoiled, their wicked laughter turning to cries of pain as they felt the searing heat of divine justice.

But they were not so easily defeated. With a wicked grin, they launched another assault, their attacks growing more ferocious with each passing moment. Yet Uriel remained resolute, his faith in the light of righteousness burning brighter than ever before.

AL'GID AND RALGIS THE FALLEN TWINS

In a final, decisive strike, Uriel unleashed the full force of his power, engulfing the fallen twins in a blaze of yellow fire and lightning. With a deafening roar, they were consumed by the flames, their malevolent presence extinguished once and for all.

As the smoke cleared and the echoes of battle faded into the ether, Uriel stood victorious, his wings of yellow flames burning brightly against the backdrop of the celestial heavens. And though the fallen twins had been vanquished, their defeat served as a reminder that the light of righteousness would always triumph over the darkness of deceit.

After his fierce battle with the twins, Uriel flies to Earth to join Haniel, pursuing Esheth toward Earth, who faked her defeat on Venus. "Haniel, have you found her yet? No, she melted and vanished," Haniel reported."Praise be to God, I barely escaped mercury facing Ral'gis and Al'gid at the same time, but by the power of Our lord's spirit, Ral'gis and Al'gid were vanquished," Uriel exclaimed! "We don't have much time to know what damage she could do with her lava, not to mention she's the sister of Satana, the queen of the Abyss," Haniel replied frantically.

Eisheth descends to Earth, her molten iron plasma form shimmering as she lands near the entrance to the Abyss. Haniel stands in her path, her wings outstretched, ready for battle.

Eisheth: (smirking) Step aside, Haniel. You cannot stop me.

Haniel: (raising her sword) You will not pass, Eisheth. Return to the darkness where you belong.

Eisheth: (laughing coldly) The darkness is where I thrive, but I have unfinished business here. (Her form flickers, and the ground sizzles beneath her.)

With a swift motion, Eisheth lunges at Haniel. The two clash, molten iron against celestial fire. Sparks fly as their powers collide.

Haniel: (gritting her teeth) I will not let you reach the Abyss.

Eisheth: (with a snarl) You are a brave but foolish little angel.

Eisheth unleashes a wave of molten iron plasma. Haniel blocks it with her sword, but the force pushes her back.

Haniel: (determined) I will fight until my last breath.

Eisheth: (smirking) So be it.

The battle rages, a dance of light and darkness. Eventually, Eisheth gains the upper hand, striking Haniel down. She stands over the fallen angel, her eyes glowing with triumph.

Eisheth: (coldly) Now, I will have my reunion.

Eisheth strides towards the Abyss, her form shifting to blend with the shadows. She descends into the depths, where the air grows thicker with sulfur, and the cries of the damned echo around her. Finally, she arrives at a grand, dark throne room. Satan and Satana await her.

Satan: (with a slow smile) Sister, you have returned.

Eisheth: (bowing slightly) Brother, it has been too long.

Satana: (with a sultry smile) Welcome back, Eisheth. The Abyss has missed you.

Eisheth: (smiling wickedly) The Abyss is my home. And it is good to be home.

Satan: (leaning forward) Tell us, sister, what brings you to us

FALLEN ANGEL YAMI

now?

Eisheth: (with a dark glint in her eyes) I seek power, and there is much to be done. The celestial realm must be reminded of our strength.

Satana: (clapping her hands) A family reunion with a purpose. How delightful.

Satan: (nodding) Then let us plot and plan. The heavens will tremble before us.

The three figures laugh, their voices blending into a chilling symphony that echoes through the Abyss.

Eisheth: (grinning) Let the world burn.

The camera pans out, showing the dark, endless expanse of the Abyss as the family of darkness prepares for their next move.

Eisheth hovers above the farmland, her form crackling with molten iron plasma. Her eyes gleam with sinister intent as she raises her hands, unleashing torrents of destructive energy. The crops ignite instantly, the fire spreading with unnatural speed.

Eisheth: (laughing maniacally) Let the world starve! Avalaria shall burn!

The flames roar, devouring everything in their path. The horizon is a wall of fire, advancing relentlessly.

In the war room, President Blackwell and General Stormheart stare at a map of Avalaria, where red markers indicate the spread of the fires. The atmosphere is tense, filled with the acrid smell of smoke.

President Blackwell: (slamming his fist on the table) How did this happen? We were winning the war!

General Stormwell: (grimly) We prepared for every conventional attack, but this… (gestures to the map) This is beyond anything we anticipated.

President Blackwell: (desperately) What can we do? We can't fight fire with bullets.

General Stormheart: (resolute) We need to call in Haniel. Only a celestial force can counter this.

Haniel descends from the heavens, her wings glowing with divine light. She surveys the burning landscape, her expression one of steely determination.

Haniel: (to herself) Eisheth, you will not destroy this world.

She flies towards the epicenter of the destruction, where Eisheth stands amidst the inferno, her laughter echoing through the flames.

Haniel: (shouting) Eisheth! Your reign of terror ends now!

Eisheth: (turning, smirking) Haniel, how noble of you to join me. Are you here to save these pitiful mortals?

Haniel: (drawing her flaming sword) I am here to stop you.

The two angels clash, light against darkness, their powers shaking the very ground. The intensity of their battle creates shockwaves, extinguishing and igniting fires with every blow.

Eisheth: (taunting) You can't stop me, Haniel. I will burn this world to ashes!

Haniel: (determined) As long as I stand, there is hope!

Their fight escalates, the landscape around them a chaotic mix of searing heat and blinding light.

President Blackwell addresses the nation from the White House, his face weary but resolute.

President Blackwell: (solemnly) My fellow citizens, we face an unprecedented crisis. Our food supplies are under attack, and fires rage across our land. But we will not succumb to despair. We will fight, and we will prevail.

The camera pans out to show the devastated farmlands, now a war zone of celestial proportions. Fires still burn, but there is a glimmer of hope as Haniel's light pushes back against the darkness.

After an intense battle, Haniel stands victorious over a defeated Eisheth, who lies weakened and bound by celestial chains.

Eisheth: (weakly) You… cannot… stop what has begun…

Haniel: (firmly) The world will heal, Eisheth. Your darkness will not prevail.

Haniel raises her sword and, with a final, blinding flash of light, banishes Eisheth back to the abyss. The fires begin to subside, and the land slowly starts to cool.

In the following days, the people of Avalaria come together to rebuild their lives. President Blackwell and General Stormheart oversee relief efforts, their faces lined with exhaustion but filled with determination.

President Blackwell: (to the crowd) We have endured much, but we are not defeated. We will restore our farms, our homes, and our way of life. Together, we will rise from the ashes.

The scene closes with Haniel watching over Avalaria from the heavens, her presence a beacon of hope for the future.

Haniel: (whispering to the wind) Be strong, Avalaria. The light will always return.

Jezebel strides through the charred remains of the forest, her green dress a stark contrast against the blackened landscape. She finds Eisheth amidst the ruins, her form still glowing with molten iron plasma.

Jezebel: (angrily) Aunt Eisheth! What have you done?

Eisheth: (coldly) I did what was necessary. Humanity must be punished.

Jezebel: (furiously) By destroying nature? By burning the forests and the farms? This is madness!

Eisheth: (with a sneer) You always were too sentimental, Jezebel. Nature is a small sacrifice for the greater plan.

Jezebel: (brandishing her axes) I will not stand by and watch you destroy what I hold dear. There must be another way!

Eisheth: (mockingly) You think you can stop me? You are nothing compared to my power.

The two clash, Jezebel's agility and skill, with her axes matching Eisheth's brute strength and plasma attacks. Their battle is fierce, shaking the ground and sending sparks flying. Eventually, they break apart, panting.

Jezebel: (breathing heavily) This isn't getting us anywhere. We need to settle this with Satana.

Eisheth: (nodding reluctantly) Very well. Let's see what my sister has to say.

Eisheth and Jezebel enter the shadowy realm where Satana resides. The realm is a dark, ethereal place, filled with swirling mists and faint whispers. Astana, a figure of serene power, sits on a throne of obsidian, her presence commanding and wise.

Satana: (calmly) Eisheth, Jezebel. To what do I owe this unexpected visit?

Jezebel: (urgently) Mother, Eisheth is destroying the natural world with her attacks. We cannot let this continue.

Eisheth: (defiantly) Humanity must be punished, sister. They have brought this upon themselves.

Satana: (thoughtfully) And yet, destroying nature itself is a harsh and reckless path, Eisheth. Tell me, what do you truly seek?

Eisheth: (bitterly) I seek to remind them of our power, to bring them to their knees.

Satana: (sighing) There are other ways to achieve our goals, ways that do not involve such wanton destruction.

Jezebel: (imploringly) Mother, there must be a balance. We can make humanity suffer without annihilating the natural world.

Satana: (nodding) Jezebel speaks with wisdom. We must be strategic, not merely destructive.

Eisheth: (frustrated) And what do you propose, Astana?

Satana: (rising from her throne) We will sow discord and fear, but we will leave the natural world intact. Humanity will face the consequences of their actions without the need for such catastrophic measures.

Eisheth: (reluctantly) Very well, sister. I will follow your counsel for now.

Jezebel: (relieved) Thank you, Mother. We must protect what is left of our world.

Satana: (with a faint smile) Go now, and remember that our true strength lies not just in destruction but in our ability to outthink and outmaneuver our enemies.

Back in Avalaria, Jezebel and Eisheth stand on the edge of the forest. The fires have been extinguished, and new green shoots are beginning to appear among the ashes.

Eisheth: (grudgingly) You were right, Jezebel. There is still beauty left to protect.

Jezebel: (smiling) We can make them suffer without destroying everything we hold dear. Together.

Eisheth: (nodding) Together, then. Let's show humanity the true meaning of fear.

The scene ends with Jezebel and Eisheth standing side by side, looking out over the recovering land, united in their resolve to take a more calculated and strategic approach to their vendetta against humanity.

In the heart of the forest, Lilith and Orpheus stand before their coven, a group of witches and wizards gathered around a bonfire. The air crackles with energy as they prepare for their ritual.

Lilith: (raising her hands) My sisters and brothers, we have endured great suffering at the hands of Malphas and his demon lords. They turned our sacred sanctuary into a prison, a place of execution for the innocent.

Orpheus: (stepping forward) But no longer. Tonight, we reclaim our power. Tonight, we seek our revenge.

The coven cheers, their voices a chorus of defiance. Lilith and Orpheus begin to chant, their words weaving a powerful spell that fills the air with dark, shimmering energy.

In the dark castle of Malphas, the demon lords gather, oblivious to the impending attack. The atmosphere is tense, filled with the sounds of chains and distant screams.

Malphas: (smirking) The coven served its purpose well. The gods' people are no more.

Belial: (laughing) Indeed. They were fools to trust those witches and wizards.

Suddenly, the room darkens, and a cold wind sweeps through. Lilith and Orpheous appear, surrounded by their coven, their eyes burning with anger.

Lilith: (coldly) Malphas, your time of reckoning has come.

Malphas: (snarling) You dare challenge me, witch?

Orpheus: (firmly) We dare, and we will prevail.

A fierce battle ensues, magic against dark power. The coven unleashes spells of fire, ice, and lightning while the demon lords retaliate with infernal might. The air is filled with explosions of energy and cries of pain.

Lilith faces off against Malphas, her eyes glowing with determination. Orpheus duels with Behemoth, their magic clashing violently.

Malphas: (taunting) You think your petty magic can defeat me?

Lilith: (smirking) It's not just my magic, Malphas. It's my rage.

She casts a powerful spell, encasing Malphas in a prison of thorns that tighten with every struggle. Meanwhile, Orpheus uses his mastery of elements to trap Behemoth in a vortex of ice and fire.

Orpheus: (shouting) Coven, now!

The coven combines their powers, creating a massive surge of energy that engulfs the remaining demon lords. Bak'Tor, Belial, and Beelzebub are consumed by the inferno, their screams echoing through the night.

With the demon lords defeated, the castle begins to crumble. Lilith and Orpheus stand victorious, their coven surrounding them.

Lilith: (breathing heavily) It is done. The demons have paid for their crimes.

Orpheus: (placing a hand on her shoulder) We have reclaimed our power, our freedom.

The coven members cheer, their voices filled with relief and triumph. The first light of dawn breaks through the darkness, symbolizing a new beginning.

Lilith: (looking out at the rising sun) This is not just revenge. This is justice.

Orpheus: (nodding) And now, we rebuild. Stronger, together.

The scene fades as the coven leaves the ruins of the castle, their spirits lifted, ready to face the future with newfound strength and unity.

Satan sits on his throne, his presence filling the room with an oppressive aura. One by one, the summoned leaders enter Malphas and his Eclipse Army, the demon lords, Lilith and Orpheous with their coven, Jezebel with her forest army, and Eisheth. They stand before Satan, uneasy under his fiery gaze.

Satan: (with a booming voice) Enough! I have watched as you turned on each other, forgetting our true enemies—humans and angels.

The gathered forces exchange nervous glances, knowing they have erred.

Satan: (standing, his eyes blazing) Malphas, Bak'Tor, Belial, Beelzebub, Behemoth—your armies squabble and weaken. Lilith, Orpheous—your coven seeks revenge not for our cause but for personal slights. Jezebel, Eisheth—you wage wars over nature and pride, not for our grand design.

He steps forward, his presence more imposing than ever.

Satan: (reprimanding) You have all disobeyed orders, deviated from the plan. This ends now. You will remember your purpose.

His voice grows even darker, resonating with power.

Satan: (with authority) We prepare for the final battle against humanity. We will crush their spirits, just as we did the first capital. This is not a time for petty squabbles or personal vendettas. We unite and destroy.

He raises his hand, summoning a vision of the human world, cities ripe for conquest and destruction.

Satan: (with a sinister smile) Look at them. Weak. Divided. They are not prepared for the force we will unleash.

Eisheth: (humbly) We will not fail you again, my lord.

Jezebel: (nodding) Our armies will be ready.

Lilith: (with resolve) The coven will stand united under your command.

Malphas: (bowing) The Eclipse Army will march at your command, supreme one.

Satan: (sternly) Good. Now, return to your realms. Prepare your forces. Forge your weapons. The final battle approaches, and we will bring humanity to its knees.

He glares at each leader, ensuring they understand the gravity of their mission.

Satan: (with finality) No more squabbles. No more defiance. We are one force, one purpose. Dismissed.

The leaders nod, a newfound determination in their eyes and leave to prepare. The scene ends with Satan standing alone, the vision of the human world still flickering before him, a dark smile playing on his lips.

Satan: (to himself) Soon, they will know the true meaning of fear.

Yami, a formidable dark angel with black flaming wings and a switch glaive, teams up with the demon Judas, who has languished in the abyss since his betrayal of Jesus thousands of years ago. Together, they take on human form and infiltrate the ranks of Avalaria's Sentinel army. Their mission was to subtly subvert and undermine the army's strength and morale, weakening their forces in preparation for the final apocalyptic battle. As they weave their dark influence, the fate of Avalaria hangs in the balance, teetering on the edge of an impending war between the forces of light and darkness.

The night is thick with fog, the moon hidden behind dense clouds. Yami, the dark angel with black flaming wings, stands beside Judas, a demon cloaked in a tattered robe, his eyes glowing with malevolent fire. They have taken on human forms, appearing as hooded figures to any passerby. In the distance, the lights of Avalarias' fortress flicker.

Yami: (Voice low and gravely) We must move swiftly, Judas. The Sentiel's army grows stronger by the day.

Judas: (A slow, malevolent chuckle) Patience, Yami. We've waited millennia in the abyss. A few more hours won't hurt. Besides, subversion requires finesse.

Yami: (Nods, though his fiery wings flicker with impatience) True. We must be like shadows, slipping through their ranks unnoticed. Have you located the weak links within their forces?

Judas: (Smirking) Indeed. I've marked several key soldiers ripe for corruption. Their minds are fragile, burdened with doubt and fear. They will crumble with the right... persuasion.

Yami: (A dark glint in his eyes) Excellent. We shall sow discord and mistrust. When the time is right, Avalarias will fall from within. Lead the way.

They move silently through the forest, their human forms blending into the darkness. As they approach the outskirts of the fortress, Yami gestures to a group of soldiers gathered around a campfire.

Yami: (In a whisper) There. They look weary. This is our chance.

Judas steps forward, his voice shifting to a soothing yet sinister tone as he speaks to the soldiers.

Judas: (With an air of concern) Good evening, soldiers. You look troubled. Is everything alright?

One of the soldiers, a young man with dark circles under his eyes, looks up, startled but weary.

Soldier: Who are you? You don't look like one of us.

Judas: (Smiling benignly) We are but humble travelers seeking refuge from the harsh night. But tell me, why such long faces? Surely, the mighty Sentiel's army has nothing to fear.

Another soldier, older and more grizzled, snorts derisively.

Grizzled Soldier: Fear? Hmph. It's not the enemy we fear. It's the endless battles, the constant vigilance. Sometimes I wonder if this war will ever end.

Yami: (Stepping forward, his voice carrying a hypnotic quality) Every war must end. But at what cost? Perhaps... there are ways to hasten that end. Ways that do not require such suffering.

Young Soldier: (Suspicious but intrigued) What do you mean?

Judas: (His eyes glowing softly in the firelight) There are... alternatives. Choices that can lead to peace if only one has the courage to take them.

The soldiers exchange uneasy glances, the seed of doubt planted. Yami and Judas withdraw into the shadows, their mission to weaken the army's resolve well underway.

Yami: (To Judas, once they are out of earshot) They will begin to question everything. We shall return to fan the flames of their doubt. Soon, Avalarias will be ripe for our final assault.

Judas: (Grinning wickedly) And then, we shall see the fall of the Sentinel. One step closer to our ultimate victory.

They disappear into the darkness, leaving behind the faint echo of their sinister laughter.

Yami and Judas sabotaged equipment, hacked systems, and gave false orders to scramble their forces, then returned to the abyss.

"My Lord Judas and I managed to cause chaos in their forces and scramble a large portion of their comms," Yami reported.

Satan replies, "Well done, I didn't even need to ask you and did more the rest of my whole army."

Yes, lord of Darkness we are honoured to serve you and time remember , I was the only one who betrayed Jesus so long a go to prove my allegiance to you, Judas pleaded.

Satan: "Yes , I'm impressed by the loyalty to cause of darkness and I will now reward you and the others for your hard work, everyone will receive a increase in rank according to their work. Then all of you need to prepare for the Battle of this age!

CHAPTER 9

Dis-Connected

So do not fear, for I am with you; do not be dismayed, for I am your God. I will strengthen you and help you; I will uphold you with my righteous right hand. -Isaiah 41:10

In the Second Heaven called the Universe, where light and darkness wage an eternal struggle, a dire mission has been decreed. Raphael, a mighty archangel clad in green-gold armor, his spear wreathed in green heavenly flames, is dispatched to an icy planet of unimaginable cold. His mission is to confront and vanquish Azreck, an ancestral fallen angel whose body is made of ice and silver, wielding formidable ice powers and an icy sword.

The icy planet looms ahead, a desolate wasteland of perpetual frost. Raphael's luminous form cuts through the void, his wings blazing with divine energy. He lands on the planet's surface, the extreme cold making the air crackle around him.

Raphael: (Surveying the frozen landscape) This forsaken place reeks of Azreck's presence. The cold is a reflection of his heart.

A distant howl echoes through the icy canyons, and Raphael grips his spear tighter, the green flames flaring brighter.

Raphael: (Calling out into the frozen wasteland) Azreck! Show yourself! Face the judgment you have long evaded!

There is a long silence, then the ground trembles as a figure emerges from the ice, tall and imposing. Azreck steps forward, his body shimmering with an eerie light, his ice sword reflecting the cold fire in his eyes.

Azreck: (His voice a chilling whisper) Raphael, the shining one. Have you come to bask in the beauty of my kingdom?

Raphael: (Firmly) I have come to end your reign of frost and terror. Your time is over, Azreck.

Azreck: (Laughing coldly) You think you can banish me with your heavenly flames? This realm is my domain. Here, my power is absolute.

Raphael: (With determination) The light of Heaven pierces all darkness, and no ice can withstand the fire of the divine.

Raphael charges his spear blazing, and Azreck counters with a swing of his ice sword. The impact sends shockwaves through the air, ice cracking and shattering beneath them. Their battle is a clash of elemental forces: fire and ice, light and shadow.

Azreck: (Striking with his sword, creating a flurry of ice shards) You cannot win, Raphael. The cold will consume you.

Raphael: (Dodging and countering with a thrust of his spear) The warmth of Heaven's grace will melt your icy heart, Azreck!

They exchange blows, each strike lighting up the frozen wasteland. Raphael's spear cuts through the ice while Azreck's sword attempts to extinguish the green flames. The planet itself seems to shudder under their conflict.

Azreck: (Summoning a blizzard to obscure Raphael's vision) You are persistent, angel, but this storm will be your end!

Raphael: (His voice is booming through the storm.) I will not falter. Your blizzards are but a breeze compared to the might of Heaven!

With a surge of divine energy, Raphael dispels the blizzard, his spear glowing ever brighter. He leaps forward, aiming for Azreck's heart. Azreck parries, but the force of Raphael's strike sends him reeling.

Azreck wounded and struggling, summons a massive ice wall to shield himself. Raphael stands before it, his spear blazing, ready to deliver the final blow.

Azreck: (Desperation in his voice) You… you cannot destroy me, Raphael! I am eternal!

Raphael: (Resolute) No evil is eternal, Azreck. The light always prevails.

Raphael channels his divine power, his spear glowing with an intensity that makes the ice around him melt. With a mighty thrust, he pierces the ice wall, shattering it and driving his spear into Azreck's chest.

ARCH- ANGEL MICHEAL

Azreck: (Gasping as he feels the spear's divine fire consuming him) No… this cannot be…

Raphael: (Solemnly) Rest now, fallen one. May your soul find peace in the light.

Azreck's form begins to dissolve, the ice melting away as the silver turns to vapor. The cold that gripped the planet started to fade, and it was replaced by a gentle warmth.

Raphael stands alone in the melting wasteland, his spear's flames dimming. The once icy planet begins to thaw, revealing the beauty beneath the frost.

Raphael: (Looking up to the heavens) It is done. The light has triumphed once more.

He spreads his wings and ascends, leaving the planet to heal and reclaim its former glory. The celestial balance is restored, and Raphael returns to the divine realms, ready for whatever challenges lie ahead.

In the heavens, Raphael kneels before the divine throne, his spear now resting by his side.

The Lord of Hosts: (Resonating with warmth and authority) You have done well, Raphael. The light shines ever brighter because of your courage.

Raphael: (Humbly) It is my honor to serve and my duty to uphold the light, God of Creation.

The Heavens rejoice, their guardians return, ever vigilant and ever ready to defend against the encroaching darkness.

In a realm where shadows reign and light is scarce, a sinister plot unfolds. The Lawless One, son of the Darklord, has risen to power. His mission is to ensure the dominion of Baal, a chief ancestral fallen angel who rules over the asteroid belt. Under the Lawless One's command, a coven of dark sorcerers is tasked with building a grand statue of Baal, compelling all followers of Satan to worship it. Their ultimate goal is to bring the world under Baal's dark authority.

In a desolate, crumbling cathedral, the Lawless One stands before a gathering of hooded figures. His presence exudes malice and power, his eyes burning with unholy fire.

Lawless One:(His voice echoing through the hall) Brothers **and sisters of the coven, the time has come to raise our master, Baal, to his rightful place of power.**

Lilith:(Stepping forward, bowing) What is your command, my lord?

Lawless One: (With a sinister smile) We shall construct a grand statue, an idol of Baal. It will be a symbol of his might and our devotion. Once it is completed, we will force the world to worship him and, thus, bring all under his dark dominion.

Coven Member: (Nervously) But, my lord, how will we compel the world to follow us?

Lawless One: (Eyes gleaming) Fear and power, my friend. We will spread chaos, and in their despair, they will turn to Baal for salvation. Begin the construction immediately.

CHIEF FALLEN ANGEL ASMODEUS

In the heart of a dark forest, the coven works tirelessly, their chants filling the air with a foreboding presence. The statue of Baal begins to take shape, towering and menacing.

Lilith:(Directing the construction) Place the sigils carefully. Every detail must be perfect to channel Baal's power.

As the final piece is put in place, the sky darkens, and a storm brews. Lightning strikes the statue, and it begins to glow with an eerie light.

Lawless One:(Raising his arms in triumph)* It is done! Behold the might of Baal! Soon, all will bow before him!

Orpheus: (Awestruck) The power... it's overwhelming.

Lawless One: (With determination) And it will be our weapon. Prepare the rituals. We shall unleash terror upon the world and demand their submission.

In cities across the globe, natural disasters strike with unprecedented fury. Earthquakes, storms, and fires ravage the land. Panic spreads, and amidst the chaos, the image of Baal appears in the sky.

News Anchor in Sanctaria: (On television) Unexplainable disasters are occurring worldwide. Authorities are at a loss, and panic is spreading.

In a darkened room, a small group of people watches the broadcast. Among them is a defiant figure, Haniel, a former member of the coven who renounced the darkness.

Sophia:(Resolutely) This is the work of the Lawless One and his coven. We must stop them.

Sophia: (Skeptically)How? They are too powerful.

Sophia: (Determined) We must find the statue and destroy it. Without it, Baal's influence will wane.

Sophia, Jophiel, Haniel, Costello, Esther, and Ralphael team up to infiltrate the forest, moving stealthily toward the statue. The air is thick with dark energy, and the coven is on high alert.

Esther:(Whispering) There it is. The statue.

Costello: (Nodding) We must act quickly. Distract the coven while I perform the counter-ritual.

Costello, Jophiel, Esther, Uriel, and Ralphael create a diversion, drawing the coven's attention. Haniel approaches the statue, her hands glowing with a faint, golden light as she begins the counter-ritual.

Lawless One: (Noticing the disruption, shouting) Intruders! Stop them!

Lilith: (Rushing towards Haniel) You will not defile our master's image! Silly Angels, you've failed to stop us so far.

Sophia: (Standing firm, her voice filled with resolve) I renounced the darkness, and I will not let it consume the world in the name of Jesus Christ.

As Haniel and her fellow Arch-angels complete the cleansing, a brilliant light envelops the statue. The ground shakes, and the statue begins to crack. Then Raphael, Uriel, Jophiel, Esther, and Costello hold up their weapons.

ARCH- ANGEL RAPHAEL

The statue crumbles and a deafening roar echoes through the forest. The dark energy dissipates, and the disasters around the world begin to subside. The coven members flee in terror as the Lawless One falls to his knees, defeated.*

Lawless One: (Desperately) No... this cannot be... Baal!

Sophia: (Stepping forward, her voice calm and powerful) The light will always triumph over darkness. Your reign ends here.

Uriel: (Approaching Haniel) We did it. The world is free from Baal's grasp.

Jophiel: (Solemnly) This is just one victory. We must remain vigilant. The darkness will always seek to return, but as long as we stand together, we can keep it at bay.

The world begins to heal from the chaos, and Haniel and the other Arch-Angels work to rebuild what was lost. The statue of Baal lies in ruins, a testament to the power of courage and unity against overwhelming darkness.

In the eternal battle between light and dark, it is the courage of a few that can change the fate of many. The fall of Baal is a reminder that even in the darkest times, hope and resolve can lead to a brighter future.

Raphael brings his healing energy the fix the damage the Evil ones had inflicted with their abomination to the Lord mocking him with a false idol. He resolutely spoke with authority and power reversing any evil affects. Raphael also heal the wound of his fellow Arch-Angels deep cut, scratches and damage to their armor was instantly made new by the power of the Most high God that gave Raphael these powers. He also healed Sentinel soldiers and other injured and sick people.

Jophiel used her fire powers to evaporate flood waters and her ice powers to put out fires. As she flew across the earth she sang songs of praise to the Lord for their victories and to strengthen her faith in her creator and determination to win the battle against the Forces of the Abyss. Her voice echoed the praises and glory of The throughout all the earth. Even theough evil still continue his mercy and grace sustains us every day until the end of time.

Uriel Displays God's glorious thunder and lighting. He use it the restore the communication systems of The Avalarian forces

and the damages power grid of the destroyed capital of Avaland. Now The sabotage of Yami and Judas was undone by the mighty Uriel. Uriel a true guardian of righteousness striking down evil where ever ith appears.

Sophia, the angel of immense wisdom, Speaks with the leaders of Avalria and imparts heavenly wisdom on issues that have bogged man for centuries. The officials were stunned by her knowledge and problem-solving skills and wanted her to work for them, but she refused. I work for God on your behalf. Sophia spreads wisdom around the world heavily, and the fear of the Lord is the beginning of knowledge, which all comes from God Almighty. Sophia's mighty voice echoes across the earth, singing songs of worship to the King of Heaven. She knows the battle between evil and good won't end any time soon, but she treads forward to protect humanity at any cost and smack evil out of any illegal place.

FALLEN – ANGEL AZRECH

Haniel is all her beauty and brings the special love and warmth of God to those who are troubled in heart and mind. She brings the Fiery vengeance of God to all of his enemies with her giant Glaming wings blazing in God's glory, and her twin flaming swords slay thousands of demons and all kinds of wicked people. She prays continually in her heart for humanity's salvation and the righteous's victory. She will always defend the innocent and weak in any realm by the Power of The Holy Spirit of God.

Costello an angelic hero elegantly brings the grace of God to the church and world. Every where Costello feet tread she speads the light of God that covers her being. No demon can escape her light though they try to flee, they will melt like wax. Costello give messages of God to the church and even change into human form to worship The lord of glory with humanity. Her Sword of light slice the even the thickest darkness with ease.

Esther, an amazing Angleic heroine, commands an army of specialized angelic soldiers equipped with a guan dao dawned in blazing bright rose red flames from heaven. The fury of her fur makes demons freeze and panic; the fire scorches their evil flesh, melting wickedness away. The way she swings her guan dao is like an elegant dance to her creator while destroying Satan's minions one by one. She is a brave, angelic hero ready for any challenge from the evil ones. Humanity must survive, and she will do her part for the sake of Heaven.

Ena Katsumi is the beautiful battle star of God with her silky long black hair and purple and gold armor, elegantly dressed with a purple scarf draped over her armor, a prayer shawl used to pray to her creator humbly. She is loving toward humanity and is full of mercy and kindness. She hates evil and wickedness. She works in the shadow like a spy helping Sentinel. Most of her work goes unnoticed, but the impact is incalculable. She hides the true extent of her angelic power to remain in position for the final battle. Before she became an angelic warrior, she was a seraph Angel flinging around God's throne, worshiping with a multitude of other angels, and volunteered at the beginning of this conflict. She believes she can live up to the same standard as the archangels in time. Defending humanity is always on her mind as she knows God's love for his people.

In the celestial realms, the balance of power hangs by a thread. Baal, a mighty ancestral fallen angel made of asteroid rock, has emerged from the shadows to sow chaos in the universe. Gabriel, an archangel with flaming blue wings and a blue flaming sword, is tasked with hunting down this formidable foe. Accompanying him was Hilbert, his secondary weapon, a halberd. a warrior angel clad in gold, white, and blue armor, his form wreathed in blue flames. Together, they embark on a perilous mission to stop

ARCH- ANGEL GABRIEL

Baal and restore peace.

In the heavenly council chamber, a radiant light bathes the room. Gabriel stands before the Divine Throne, his wings blazing with blue fire. Hilbert stands beside him, resolute and ready.

The Lord : (Echoing through the chamber) Gabriel, the time has come. Baal has risen, and his presence threatens the harmony of the cosmos.

Gabriel: (Bowing his head) We are ready, my Lord. Where shall we find this fallen one?

Jesus: (Solemnly) Baal resides in the asteroid belt, hidden among the celestial debris. His form is as resilient as the rock he inhabits. You must seek him out and bring him to justice.

Gabriel: (Clenching his fist in determination) We will not fail. Baal will be brought to justice.

Gabriel soars through the void, the asteroid belt sprawling before them. The debris field is vast and treacherous, each rock a potential hiding place for Baal.

Gabriel: (Scanning the surroundings) This place is a labyrinth. Finding Baal here will be like searching for a needle in a haystack.

Gabriel: (With unwavering confidence) Trust in the mission, Gabriel. The light of God will guide me.

Suddenly, a massive asteroid shifts, revealing a hulking figure made of rock and dark energy. Baal emerges, his eyes glowing with malevolence.

Baal: (His voice like grinding stone) Gabriel, I knew you would come. But you will find no victory here.

Gabriel: (Drawing his blue flaming sword) Your reign of terror ends now, Baal. Face the light and be judged.

Gabriel: (Blue Flames intensifying around him) We will not let you spread your darkness any further!

The battle begins with a furious exchange of blows. Gabriel's sword clashes against Baal's rocky form, sending sparks flying. Gabriel's Halbert unleashes waves of blue fire, attempting to weaken Baal's defenses.

Baal: (Laughing mockingly) You think your flames can harm me? I am as eternal as the cosmos itself!

Gabriel: (Striking with precision) The light of Heaven can pierce any darkness, Baal. You cannot escape your fate.

Baal retaliates, swinging massive fists of stone and creating shockwaves that send asteroids flying. Gabriel and Hilbert dodged and countered, and their teamwork was seamless and effective.

Gabriel: (Shouting over the din of battle) We need to find a way to weaken him. His rock form is too resilient!

Gabriel: (Nodding) Focus on his joints. Even the strongest stone has its weak points.

They adjust their strategy, targeting the joints and crevices in Baal's form. Gradually, cracks begin to appear, but Baal's power is formidable, and he fights back with relentless fury.

As the battle rages on, Gabriel receives a divine vision, showing a celestial artifact hidden deep within the asteroid belt that can amplify their powers. He communicates this to Hilbert telepathically

Gabriel: (Through their mental link) Hilbert, there is a way. Follow my lead.

They break away from the fight, leading Baal on a chase through the asteroid field. They navigate through tight spaces and treacherous terrain, finally arriving at an ancient celestial temple embedded in an asteroid.

Gabriel: (In awe) This place... it's magnificent. Blessed be the Lord who stretched out heavens!

Gabriel: (Urgently) I don't have much time. The artifact is within. I must activate it.

They enter the temple, and at its center, a glowing orb pulses with divine energy. Gabriel and Hilbert place their hands on it, and their forms are enveloped in a blinding light. Their flames burn brighter, and their strength increases tenfold.

Baal: (Bursting into the temple, enraged) What have you done?!

Gabriel: (Eyes blazing with newfound power) We have unlocked the true power of the light. Prepare to face your end, Baal.

With their enhanced powers, Gabriel and Hilbert reengage Baal. Their attacks are faster, stronger, and more precise. The celestial energy flows through them, their flames turning white-hot.

Baal: (Roaring in pain and fury as their attacks penetrate his defenses) No! This cannot be! I am invincible!

Gabriel: (Delivering a powerful blow) Nothing is invincible against the light!

Gabriel's powers create a massive beam of divine energy. They direct it at Baal, and it pierces through his rocky form, shattering him into countless fragments.

Gabriel: (As Baal disintegrates) Return to the void, Baal. Your darkness has no place in the light.

The fragments of Baal dissipate, and the asteroid belt becomes calm once more. The celestial temple's light fades, and Gabriel stands victorious.

Back in the heavenly realms, Gabriel and Hilbert kneel before the Divine Throne, their mission accomplished.

God: (Resonating with warmth and pride) You have done well, my faithful warriors. The cosmos is safe once more.

Gabriel: (Humbly) It was an honor to serve, my Lord. We will remain vigilant, always ready to defend the light.

Micheal: (Resolute) Baal is defeated, but the battle against darkness continues. We will be ready.

The celestial realms rejoice as the balance of power is restored. Gabriel and Micheal, their spirits unyielding, prepared for whatever challenges the future may bring, their flames burning brightly in the eternal fight between light and darkness.

Gabriel: Michael, I beat Baal.

Michael: That's good news. I'm heading towards their chief, Asmodeus. I would double-check to make sure Baal is really dead.

Gabriel: Yes, sir, General, If he manages to slips away, I'll finish him off for good. It seems that the Demon presence has been successfully held back on Earth despite a few set backs.

Micheal: It's a rouse. They're just biding their time. Satan

FALLEN ANGEL BAAL

and his guild have become very crafty. May the grace of Yah be with us all.

Gabriel: Amen. Whatever they've planned, we'll put a stop to it. The wicked must perish.

Gabriel had believed he had defeated Baal once and for all, but he was gravely mistaken. Unknown to him, Baal had managed to hide behind an asteroid during their last battle. Now, with a sinister plan unfolding, Baal was making his way toward the moon, intending to use it as a massive weapon to annihilate Earth.

As Gabriel received the alarming news, he knew he had to act quickly. Time was running out, and the fate of the planet hung in the balance. Determined to stop Baal's catastrophic scheme, Gabriel set off in his advanced spacecraft, racing against time to intercept Baal before it was too late.

With the moon growing larger in his view, Gabriel steeled himself for the upcoming confrontation. He could see Baal's ship nearing the lunar surface, preparing to execute the devastating plan. This final battle would be the ultimate test of Gabriel's strength, courage, and determination. The stakes had never been higher, and failure was not an option.

As Gabriel closed in on Baal, he could feel the weight of his responsibility. He had to protect Earth and its inhabitants at all costs. The showdown on the moon would determine the fate of humanity, and Gabriel was ready to face Baal once more, determined to save the world from imminent destruction.

In the vast expanse of the cosmos, the eternal struggle between good and evil reaches new heights. The Archangel Michael, Heaven's most formidable warrior, is summoned to face a dire threat: Asmodeus, the king of the ancestral fallen angels, has set his sights on Earth, plotting its annihilation from his stronghold on Jupiter.

Michael descends through the swirling gases of Jupiter, his flaming orange wings blazing a path through the thick ammonia and hydrogen atmosphere. His massive, flaming great sword cuts through the dense fog, illuminating the desolate landscape below. He struggles with the harsh environment, his breath labored as he lands on the gaseous surface.

Michael: (to himself) "These conditions are worse than anticipated. But I cannot falter. Earth depends on me."

In the distance, a figure emerges from the clouds: Asmodeous, towering, and muscular, his blue wings spreading wide. His giant mace crackles with powerful blue lightning, illuminating the stormy atmosphere around him.

Asmodeus: (smirking) "Welcome, Michael. I see you've come to stop me. How noble, yet foolish."

Michael: (steadies himself, gripping his sword) "Asmodeous, your reign of terror ends here. You will not harm Earth as long as I draw breath."

The two titans rush at each other, their weapons clashing with a thunderous roar. The impact sends shockwaves through the gaseous surface, scattering clouds and revealing glimpses of the planet's roiling core beneath.

Asmodeus: (laughing, swinging his mace) "You struggle against the very elements of this world. How do you expect to defeat me?"

Michael: (dodging, countering with a fiery slash) "By the will of Heaven and the strength of my faith!"

Michael's sword strikes true, cutting through the lightning-infused air, but Asmodeous's lightning-imbued mace meets it with equal force, creating an explosive burst of energy.

The battle rages on, each clash of their weapons echoing through the thick atmosphere. Michael fights through the suffocating gases, his resolve unwavering, while Asmodeus revels in his power, the lightning from his mace growing more intense.

Asmodeus: (taunting) "Feel the power of Jupiter, Michael! This is my domain!"

Michael: (panting, eyes glowing with divine light) "Your power is nothing compared to the righteousness of Heaven!"

Summoning his remaining strength, Michael unleashes a powerful surge of divine fire, his wings blazing brighter than ever. He charges at Asmodeous with a renewed fury, his sword cutting through the thick atmosphere like a beacon of hope.

Michael's fiery assault overwhelms Asmodeous, forcing him back. The blue lightning of Asmodeous's mace begins to falter under the relentless onslaught of Michael's divine flames.

Asmodeus: (struggling, eyes widening in anger) "Impossible! You cannot defeat me!"

Michael: (voice steady, determined) "By the grace of God, I will!"

With a final, powerful strike, Michael's flaming great sword cleaves through Asmodeous's mace, shattering it into pieces. The divine flames engulf Asmodeous, burning away the corruption and weakening him significantly.

Asmodeus falls to his knees, his blue wings singed and his power diminishing. Michael stands over him, his sword blazing with holy fire.

Asmodeus: (weakly) "This… is not the end…"

Michael: (firmly) "It is the end of your threat to Earth. Begone, Asmodeous, and may you find redemption in the afterlife."

With a final, cleansing sweep of his sword, Michael banishes Asmodeus back into the depths of the cosmos. The stormy atmosphere of Jupiter begins to calm, the divine light of Michael's victory spreading across the planet.

Michael, exhausted but triumphant, spreads his wings and ascends back through the gases, leaving Jupiter behind. He looks back one last time before setting his sights on Earth, a small but resilient blue planet, safe once more thanks to his unwavering resolve.

Michael: (whispering to himself) "The battle is won, but the war continues. For Earth, for Heaven, I will always stand ready."

With that, Michael disappears into the heavens, a guardian of light against the encroaching darkness.

Asmodeous: I will rise micheal You can't beat me that easy remember I was also high ranking Arch-angel our power and strength is very similar. Our battle is far from over, You angels are very arrogant thinking your allegiance to Heaven makes you invincible. That's why I joined the rebellion in the beginning of time. When God and You banished us from Heaven into the darkness of void.

Micheal: Foolish and rebellious cherub, you betrayed all of heaven, yet you preach to me?

You have already defeated foe your it's only by The Lord's mercy do you still breathe Asmodeous no matter how long it takes. I will Swear by him Who lives forever and by he who is enthroned among the Cherubims, I will stop you Asmodeous.

STATUE OF BAAL

Asmodeus blinds Michael with a burst of lightning and streaks toward Earth, leaving Michael momentarily stunned. Regaining his sight, Michael immediately gives chase, determined to stop the demon's descent. As they hurtle through the cosmos, their paths align with Mars, where an intense battle unfolds between Gabriel and Baal. The two archrivals clash with ferocious energy, their conflict sending shockwaves rippling through the Martian atmosphere. The stakes are high, and the heavens themselves seem to tremble under the weight of their struggle.

Technician 1: Sir, we've detected anomalous energy signatures above Mars. Flashes of blue and orange, along with lightning strikes.

Technician 2: It's unlike anything we've seen before. It could be celestial in nature.

Commander: Get me, General Alexander Stormheart, immediately.

Scene: General Alexander Stormheart's Office

General Stormheart: (answering the urgent call) This is Stormheart. What's the situation?

Commander: General, we've observed violent energy surges above Mars. The signatures are consistent with… well, sir, they might be celestial beings. Fallen angels, to be precise.

General Stormheart: (stunned) Fallen angels? Are you certain?

Commander: As certain as we can be. Sir, if they're heading towards Earth, it could mean an extinction-level event.

General Stormheart: Understood. I'll report this to the President immediately. Keep monitoring and alert me of any changes.

General Stormheart: Mr. President, Vice President, we have a situation. Space Command has detected what appears to be fallen angels battling above Mars. They're heading towards Earth. We believe they may team up with demons to destroy us.

President Blackwell: (grave) Fallen angels? This is unprecedented. Are we looking at an extinction-level threat?

General Stormheart: Yes, sir. We need to prepare for the worst.

Vice President Morgan: We have to alert our allies. The entire world must be prepared for this.

President Blackwell: Agreed. General, send out the alert. Inform the leaders of every nation to ready their armies and deploy all available technology and weaponry. And we must call on our people to pray for divine intervention.

President Blackwell: (on a secure video call with global leaders) Esteemed colleagues, we face an existential threat. Space Command has confirmed that fallen angels, possibly aligned with demons, are en route to Earth. This is an extinction-level event. We must unite and deploy every resource at our disposal.

Prime Minister: This is unprecedented. What are our chances?

President Blackwell: Slim, but we must try. Prepare your armies and utilize all technological and weapon advancements. And most importantly, have your people pray for mercy. We need all the help we can get, both earthly and divine.

Chancellor: We'll do whatever it takes. Our forces will be ready.

Chairman: any enemy will be defeated by our great people and regret their dangerous actions.

President Blackwell: (solemnly) Then may God help us all.

Scene: Various Locations Around the World

News Anchor: (broadcasting) In an unprecedented move, world leaders have issued a global alert, urging all nations to prepare for a possible extinction-level event. Citizens are advised to stay indoors and pray for divine intervention as military forces mobilize worldwide.

Soldier 1: (loading weapons) Did you ever think we'd be preparing to fight angels and demons?

Soldier 2: No, but if it comes to that, we'll give them everything we've got.

Soldier 1: Amen to that. And let's hope the prayers work too.

Priest: (leading a packed congregation) Let us pray, my brothers and sisters. We seek God's mercy and protection in this time of great peril.

Technician 1: General, the energy signatures are intensifying. They're getting closer.

General Stormheart: (resolute) This is it. May God be with us.

Commander: And with them. Godspeed, General.

As the world braces for the impending battle, humanity's fate hangs in the balance, a desperate prayer echoing across the globe.

All of the world leaders flew to Sanctaria, the new capital of Avalaría, where the Massive military force had been gathered months ago: anti-aircraft missiles, ballistic missiles, artillery, tanks, laser weapons, attack helicopters, a vast fleet of drones. A mighty naval submarine and destroyer battle groups and hundreds of thousands of troops are in positions all around the nation, and millions of troops are worldwide. Sanctaria was a fortress of biblical proportions.

Narrator: The world leaders have convened in Sanctaria, the fortified heart of Avalaría, transformed into a citadel of immense military power. For months, preparations have been underway, turning the capital into a fortress of biblical proportions.

General Stormheart: (addressing world leaders) Ladies and gentlemen, welcome to Sanctaria. Our defenses are ready. We have anti-aircraft missiles, ballistic missiles, artillery, tanks, laser weapons, attack helicopters, a vast fleet of drones, and a mighty naval force of submarines and destroyers. Hundreds of thousands of troops are positioned around the nation, with millions more worldwide.

President Blackwell: (grimly) This is it. Sanctaria is our last bastion. We must be ready for anything.

Prime Minister: This city is a fortress. If anything can withstand the onslaught, it's Sanctaria.

Vice President Morgan: We have gathered the best minds and the most advanced technology here. We must stand united.

Officer: (to troops) Check your equipment and stay vigilant. Remember, we're the first line of defense. Hold your positions no matter what.

THE LAWLESS ONE

Soldier 1: (loading weapon) Never thought I'd be defending against fallen angels and demons.

Soldier 2: We stand for humanity. Whatever comes, we face it together.

Pilot: (prepping helicopter) Our mission is clear. Intercept and neutralize any threats. This is our home, and we protect it.

Co-Pilot: Roger that. We've trained for this. Time to show what we can do.

Admiral: (on the bridge of a destroyer) Our fleet is positioned and ready. We hold the line at sea. No one gets through.

Captain: All systems are go. Submarines are in position. We're ready to engage on your command.

President Blackwell: (speaking to the world) Citizens of Earth, we stand at the precipice of an unparalleled challenge. Here in Sanctaria, we have gathered our strength, our technology, and our resolve. Our forces are ready, but we also need your faith and prayers. Together, we stand, and together, we shall overcome.

Priest: (leading a global prayer) Almighty God, we come before you in our hour of need. Grant us strength, courage, and protection. We pray for the brave souls defending us and for your divine intervention.

Congregation: Amen.

Technician 1: General, incoming reports. The energy signatures are now within striking distance.

General Stormheart: (steely-eyed) This is it. All units prepare for engagement. May God be with us all.

Commander: The world is watching. We stand united.

General Stormheart: (raising his voice) Soldiers of Earth, this is our moment. Stand firm, fight with all you have, and remember—we fight not just for survival but for the future of humanity.

As the forces of Sanctaria and the entire world brace for the impending assault, a palpable tension fills the air. The fate of humanity rests in the balance, with hope, technology, and faith intertwined in a desperate stand against the celestial threat.

God's Voice: (booming and omnipresent) Michael, my faithful servant, listen to my command. Give Asmodeus the key to the bottomless pit.

Michael: (confused but obedient) Lord, I do not understand, but I trust in Your wisdom and will obey.

Asmodeus: (with a triumphant grin) Finally, the key to the bottomless pit is ours. There is no stopping us now, Michael. You have failed. You have literally handed us the key to victory.

Michael: (calmly and with conviction) No, Asmodeus. The Lord knows all. His ways are higher than our ways, and His thoughts are higher than our thoughts. If He commands that you have this key, then it will surely lead to your defeat.

Asmodeus: (mocking) Defeat? You fool. You've just ensured your own destruction. Our victory is at hand.

Michael: (steadfast) As it is written, pride comes before a fall. Your arrogance will be your undoing, Asmodeus. The Lord's plan is perfect, and His justice will prevail.

Scene: Sanctaria, the New Capital of Avalaría

Narrator: Unbeknownst to the defenders of Sanctaria, the heavenly battle, and God's mysterious command have set the stage for the unfolding events on Earth. The mighty fortress stands ready, its forces prepared for the celestial onslaught.

Technician 1: General Stormheart, we've detected unusual energy readings. It looks like the celestial beings are approaching.

General Stormheart: (resolute) All units prepare for engagement. This is it. We hold the line here.

President Blackwell: (to the gathered world leaders) The moment has come. Stay strong. Our faith and unity are our greatest weapons.

Vice President Morgan: May God protect us all.

Soldier 1: (looking at the sky) Here they come. Remember, we fight for humanity. Hold your positions!

Soldier 2: (nodding) We've trained for this. We're ready. Let's show them our strength.

Asmodeus: (leading the celestial charge, holding the key) Behold, Michael! Your fortress will fall, and with it, your precious humanity.

Michael: (hovering, sword drawn) This key will not save you, Asmodeus. The Lord's will is supreme. Your pride will lead you to ruin.

Asmodeus: (laughing) We shall see, Michael. We shall see.

Pilot: (taking off in an attack helicopter) This is it. All units engage the enemy. Protect Sanctaria at all costs.

Co-Pilot: (locking targets) We're ready. Let's take them down.

Admiral: (on the bridge of a destroyer) All ships prepare to engage. Maintain formation and hold the line. No one gets through.

Captain: (monitoring radar) Targets acquired. Awaiting your command.

Admiral: Fire at will. For Sanctaria, for Earth.

The skies above Sanctaria light up with flashes of blue and orange as the forces of Heaven and Hell clash with Earth's defenders. Anti-aircraft missiles launch, drones swarm, and laser weapons sear through the air. Michael and Asmodeus engage in a fierce duel, their swords clashing with divine and infernal power.

Asmodeus: (struggling against Michael) You cannot win, Michael! The key ensures our victory!

Michael: (with unwavering faith) The Lord's plan is beyond your comprehension. Your pride will be your downfall.

Asmodeus: (angrily) Silence! You will fall today!

Narrator: Michael hands Asmodeus the key to the bottomless pit, and Asmodeus flies with unmatched speed towards an ancient volcano, a place steeped in dark history and power. This is where Aberdeen, the great dragon, emerged centuries ago in the first Eternal Battle.

Asmodeus: (landing at the edge of the volcano, holding the key aloft) Finally, the time has come. With this key, the abyss will open, and our reign will begin.

Asmodeus: (in a deep, resonant voice) By the power of the abyss, I command you to open!

The volcano trembles as a rift opens, a portal to the bottomless pit. Dark energy surges, and from the abyss emerges a host of ancient and powerful demons.

SATANA QUEEN OF THE ABYSS

Santana: (stepping forward) Brother, it has been too long. Welcome back.

Satan: (with a sinister smile) Asmodeus, you have done well. The key to the abyss… now we can unleash our true power.

Satans: (embracing Asmodeus) The universe will tremble before us.

The Lawless One: (smirking) The world has forgotten our might. It is time to remind them.

Jezebel: (with a wicked grin) We shall reclaim what is ours.

Lilith: (eyes glowing) The time for revenge has come.

Aberdeen: (towering above the others) The ancient powers shall rise again.

Leviathan: (emerging from the shadows) The seas will boil with our fury.

Orpheus: (darkly) We bring chaos and ruin.

Bak'tor: (with a growl) The armies of darkness will march.

Belial: (laughing) The mortals will fall.

Beelzebub: (wings spread wide) Our dominion will be absolute.

Behemoth: (with a roar) The land will quake beneath our might.

Python: (hissing) We will crush all opposition.

Judas: (with a sneer) Betrayal and deceit will reign supreme.

Lord Malphas Darkbane: (commanding the Eclipse army) My legions are ready. We await your command, Asmodeus.

Eisheth: (with a cold smile) The souls of the fallen will be ours.

Asmodeus: (raising the key) This key will free every fallen angel in the universe. Together, we shall unleash a darkness that will consume all.

The portal widens, and legions of demons pour forth, their roars and screams echoing across the land. The ground trembles as the ancient volcano erupts with dark energy, signaling the rebirth of an era of chaos and destruction.

Narrator: The defenders of Sanctaria, unaware of the growing threat at the ancient volcano, continue to brace for the next wave of battle.

Technician 1: General Stormheart, we're detecting massive energy surges from an ancient volcanic region. It's unlike anything we've seen before.

General Stormheart: (concerned) This can't be good. Mobilize our forces. We need to investigate and prepare for the worst.

President Blackwell: (addressing the world leaders) Another threat is emerging. We must stand ready. The battle is not yet over.

Vice President Morgan: (nodding) Our unity and faith will guide us through this dark hour.

Asmodeus: (to the assembled demons) Spread across the Earth. Bring terror and destruction. The age of darkness begins now.

The demons disperse, spreading their dark influence across the globe, while Asmodeus and the key remain at the volcano, orchestrating the next phase of their plan.

Priest: (leading a prayer) Almighty God, we call upon Your protection once more. Guide us and give us strength to face this new threat.

Congregation: Amen.

Michael: (watching from above) The darkness spreads, but the light of the Lord will prevail. I must rally the forces of Heaven.

Gabriel: (joining Michael) Together, we will fight this evil. God's will is our strength.

Michael: (resolute) Let us prepare for the final battle. The fate of humanity depends on it.

As the forces of light and darkness prepare for the ultimate confrontation, the world stands on the brink of a cataclysmic battle, with the fate of all creation hanging in the balance.

Micheal assembles his band of Arch-Angels Jophiel, Haniel, Uriel, Raphael, Gabriel, Esther, and Costello to gather for the finale.

Narrator: Michael, sensing the urgency of the growing darkness, calls upon his fellow archangels to prepare for the final, decisive battle against the forces of evil.

Michael: (standing tall, his sword gleaming) My brothers and sisters, the time has come. The darkness rises, and with it, the fate of humanity and the universe. We must be ready to fight. Jophiel, Haniel, Sophia, Uriel, Raphael, Gabriel, Esther, Costello—assemble!

Jophiel: (radiant with divine light) Michael, we stand ready. The beauty of Heaven shines within us, and we will illuminate the path to victory.

Haniel: (with serene determination) Our love and compassion will guide us through this darkness. The forces of evil cannot withstand our unity.

Sophia: (wise and resolute) The wisdom of the ages is our weapon. We shall outthink and outmaneuver our enemies.

Uriel: (fiery and fierce) The flame of justice burns within me. I will bring light to the darkest corners and cleanse the world of this evil.

Raphael: (healing and kind) I will heal the wounded and protect the innocent. Our strength lies not just in our might but in our mercy.

Gabriel: (heralding with a powerful voice) I will sound the trumpet of truth, rallying the forces of Heaven and Earth. Together, we are invincible.

Esther: (with unwavering faith) The courage of the righteous will not falter. We are the guardians of hope and faith.

Costello: (steady and brave) I will be the shield against the storm. No harm shall befall those under my protection.

Michael: (raising his sword) We face a formidable foe led by Asmodeus and his legion. They possess the key to the bottomless pit, but their pride will be their downfall. Remember, the Lord's wisdom surpasses all. His ways are higher than our ways.

Gabriel: (nodding) We have faced darkness before, but never have we been more united. The strength of our faith will see us through.

Uriel: (clenching his fist) Let them come. We will meet them with the full fury of Heaven.

Raphael: (softly) And we will heal the world in the aftermath. Every wound will be mended.

Jophiel: (smiling) The beauty of Heaven will be restored on Earth. This is our promise.

Michael: (with resolve) Then let us descend, my friends. To Sanctaria, where the final battle awaits. For the glory of Heaven, for the love of God, and for the salvation of humanity!

All Archangels: (in unison) For Heaven! For Earth! For the Lord!

Narrator: As the archangels descend, their divine light piercing through the dark clouds, the forces of Sanctaria look up with renewed hope. The final battle is about to begin, a clash of celestial and infernal powers, with the fate of all creation hanging in the balance.

Michael: (addressing the assembled armies of Heaven and Earth) Stand firm! The forces of evil approach, but we are not alone. With the Lord's strength and our unity, we shall prevail. Remember, as it is written, pride comes before a fall. Let their arrogance be their undoing.

Asmodeus: (from a distance, mocking) Come, Michael! Bring your angels! Today, we shall see who truly holds the power.

Michael: (with unwavering faith) We shall see, Asmodeus. We shall see.

The final battle commences, a symphony of light and dark, as angels and demons clash in a fight for the very soul of the universe. The air crackles with energy, and the fate of all creation hangs in the balance.

Narrator: Amidst the chaos of the final battle, a new threat emerges. Baal, a mighty fallen angel, soars into the heavens with a sinister plan to push the moon into the Earth, plunging the world into darkness.

Baal: (with a menacing grin) The time has come. I will bring eternal night to the Earth and crush the hopes of humanity.

With a tremendous force, Baal begins to move the moon, swinging it past the sun, initiating a massive eclipse. The Earth becomes shrouded in darkness.

Narrator: As the world below is cast into shadow, Gabriel, the archangel of fire, ascends with a blazing blue aura, determined to thwart Baal's destructive plan.

Gabriel: (soaring towards Baal, blue fire blazing) Baal! I will not let you bring ruin to the Earth!

Baal: (laughing darkly) Gabriel, your flames are no match for my power. Prepare to be extinguished!

Gabriel and Baal clash in a fierce battle, their powers lighting up the darkened sky. Blue fire meets demonic strength as they struggle over the fate of the moon.

Gabriel: (straining) I will not allow you to destroy everything! Feel the might of Heaven's fire!

With a mighty effort, Gabriel unleashes his full strength, enveloping Baal in blue flames. In a decisive move, he stabs Baal in the stomach with his divine blade.

Baal: (roaring in pain) No! This cannot be!

Gabriel: (with determination) Return to where you belong, Baal!

Gabriel punches Baal with all his strength, sending him hurtling back towards the asteroid belt. He quickly secures a celestial chain around Baal, binding him and preventing his return.

Gabriel: (securing the chain) By the authority of Heaven, you are bound, Baal. You will not threaten Earth again.

Narrator: As Gabriel's victory over Baal is secured, the moon slowly moves back to its rightful place, the eclipse ending. Light returns to the Earth, restoring hope to those below.

General Stormheart: (watching the sky) Look! The light returns! Gabriel has succeeded!

President Blackwell: (with renewed hope) This is a sign. We must hold our ground. The forces of Heaven are with us.

Vice President Morgan: (nodding) Our faith and resilience will see us through this battle.

Michael: (seeing Gabriel's victory) Well done, Gabriel. Your strength and courage are an inspiration to us all.

Gabriel: (returning, slightly weary but triumphant) The threat of Baal is contained. Now, let us turn our focus to the remaining forces of darkness.

Michael: (raising his sword) Onward, my brothers and sisters. The final victory is within our grasp.

With renewed determination, the archangels and the forces of Earth press forward, their spirits lifted by Gabriel's triumph. The battle rages on, but the light of Heaven shines brighter, guiding them toward the ultimate victory over the forces of darkness.

Angered by Baal's defeat, Lord Malphas Darkbane issues a dire command to his Eclipse army.

Lord Darkbane: (seething) Prepare the electric bomb infused with Asmodeus's lightning. Wipe Sanctaria off the map. Let them know the true power of darkness.

The Eclipse army swiftly prepares the devastating weapon, aiming it directly at Sanctaria.

Ena Katsumi: (kneeling in prayer, her hands clasped tightly) Almighty God, grant us strength and protection in this hour of need. Let Your light shine through the darkness.

As the missile launches, alarms blare throughout the command center. Soldiers scramble, realizing the impending doom.

General Stormheart: (shouting) Incoming missile! Everyone, take cover!

Technician 1: General, the energy readings are off the charts! We need to evacuate!

Ena Katsumi: (rising from her prayer) No, I will not let this city fall. God has a plan, and I am His instrument.

Narrator: As the missile streaks towards Sanctaria, Ena Katsumi rushes out to meet it, her heart filled with divine purpose. She transforms into her true form, a powerful seraphim angel.

Ena Katsumi: (her voice echoing with divine power) By the grace of God, I shall protect this city!

Her six wings burst into purple flames, and she draws a mighty purple flaming sword. Her armor gleams with purple, white, and gold, and a purple scarf drapes over her shoulders. Her face and hands shine like stars, embodying the power of God.

Narrator: Ena Katsumi, now in her full seraphim form, soars towards the incoming missile. Soldiers on the ground looked up in awe, not knowing that an angel had been among them.

Soldier 1: (in awe) Look! Is that… an angel?

Soldier 2: (astonished) She was one of them all along…

Ena Katsumi: I am God's battle star, and I shall defend His people!

As the missile nears, she meets it head-on, her purple flames intensifying. The electric bomb explodes with a tremendous force, but Ena's divine power shields Sanctaria. The sky lights up with a dazzling display of purple and gold as she absorbs the energy, protecting the city below.

Ena Katsumi, her six wings aflame in vivid purple fire, descends from the sky. Ena was wielding her massive purple-flaming sword, alive with the radiance of God's light. Her face and hands, formed of pure light, radiate a divine glow as she stands over a city she has just saved, having slain 10,000 demons. The Eclipse Troops scattered before her, seeing the mercy in her eyes and fearing for their lives. Yet she spares them, allowing them to flee.

A massive, Vast cityscape under a darkened sky. Ena Katsumi soars amidst the Battle, her six flaming purple wings spreading wide, her sword blazing with holy fire. Satana approaches, her once-bright wings now tarnished, followed by Jezebel, Lily, and BaK'tor.

Satana:

"So, God has sent his precious Battlestar to do His bidding? Look at you, Ena Katsumi—so bright, so… pure. Do you even remember me?" "God Replaced Me with you after we fell?!"

Ena Katsumi:

"I remember the angel you were, Satana. I remember your light, the beauty of your devotion. But that was long ago before you chose the path of darkness."

Satana (scoffs, a bitter smile forming):

"Do you think you're so different from me? Look around! This world will burn, just as I did. But unlike you, I embrace the flames."

Ena Katsumi:

"The flames of Hell and your pride have twisted your heart. Once, you represented love for light. But now, you and your followers only bring ruin. Your end is near Satana!" "Stand down and I'll Spare you!"

Jezebel (sneering as she circles Ena):

"Mercy? What does an angel like you know of mercy? You slay our kind like insects, and now you preach mercy?"

Ena: "Need I remind you, Jezebel, The Kingdom of Darkness Started this War!"

Lily (drawing her weapon):

"Ena Katsumi, you are outnumbered. You may have felled thousands, but we are the strongest of Hell. And we have no intention of bending to your God's mercy."

BaK'tor:

"All that awaits your kind is defeat, Ena. This is the end of your sanctimonious reign, Katsumi."

Ena Katsumi (raising her sword, voice steady yet compassionate):

"You mistake my words for weakness. This is your final chance. God's mercy is greater than His wrath. But if you refuse, know that I am ready."

Satana (snarling, rushing toward Ena with Jezebel, Lily, and Bachor charging beside her):

"Mercy means nothing to us! You'll die here, Battlestar of God!"

Ena's wings flare as she clashes with all four foes, her sword sending Fiery shockwaves that push them back. The city quakes with each impact.

Ena Katsumi:

"Feel this, Satana—the strength of God's will. It is not my mercy that spares you; it is His! This battle is not yours to win. Turn back or face the consequence."

The fallen ones stagger back, momentarily halted by Ena's power. They retreat, each glancing back with expressions of fear and hatred, except Satana, who glares with a mix of defiance and an old, lingering sadness.

Satana (calling back with a hint of venom):

"This isn't over, Ena. One day, you'll see—your mercy is just a chain holding you back."

In the shadows, Satana, Queen of hell, once a mighty angel of Heaven, watches Ena Katsumi. Memories flood her mind— she, too, once bore the same brilliant purple flames and wings of glory when she served God. Jealousy burns deep within her now-darkened heart, her envy becoming a fierce heat demanding vengeance. With a cry of rage, she charges, flanked by two other fallen angels and an Arch-Demon: Jezebel, Lilith, and BaK'tor. Together, they dive toward Ena, a dark tide of fury and power.

But Ena, filled with God's strength, stands firm. As they clash, a massive shockwave erupts, sending the wicked ones reeling back. The

Eclipse Troops, watching this, tremble, fearing that they will be next to fall beneath her blade.

Then, a powerful voice from above halts the battle, filling the skies with a sense of mercy and finality. God commands Ena to deliver a message to the Eclipse Troops—a final chance for repentance. Those who choose to turn from evil may yet live, joining God's side and seeking redemption. Some heed the call, laying down their weapons, their hearts turning towards the light. Others, however, remain defiant, spitting curses and holding tightly to their wickedness.

Ena Katsumi (to the scattered eclipse troops watching from afar):

"To those who still have ears to hear: Repent and return to the light! Those who remain wicked will fall. God's mercy is your final shield—choose it, or face the fate of your kind."

Some Soldiers bow their heads, filled with fear and remorse. Others snarl, refusing her words. Ena watches as they begin to disperse, sensing the weight of her words and God's command.

In silence, Ena lifts her sword once more, and with swift justice, she slays those who have refused the mercy offered to them by God.

Ena Katsumi: (with a mighty roar) In the name of Jesus, be gone!

With a powerful swing of her purple flame sword, she dispels the remaining energy, ensuring Sanctaria's safety. The explosion subsides, and the sky returns to its serene state.

Narrator: The soldiers, having witnessed Ena Katsumi's transformation and her heroic act, stand in awe and reverence.

General Stormheart: (speechless) Ena... she saved us all.

President Blackwell: (with gratitude) Truly, she is a sign of God's favor upon us.

Vice President Morgan: (inspired) Her courage and divine power give us hope. We are not alone in this fight.

Narrator: Ena Katsumi descends gently to the ground, her wings still ablaze with purple flames. She looks at her fellow soldiers with a serene smile.

Ena Katsumi: (softly) Fear not, for God is with us. Stand strong, and we shall prevail.

The soldiers, emboldened by Ena's divine presence, ready themselves for the next phase of the battle. With renewed faith and strength, they prepare to face the remaining forces of darkness.

General Stormheart: (raising his weapon) For Sanctaria! For humanity! Let's show them our true strength!

As the battle continues, the light of Heaven shines brightly, guiding the defenders of Sanctaria toward ultimate victory. Ena Katsumi, God's battle star, stands at their forefront, a beacon of hope and divine power.

Technician 2: General, our defenses are holding, but the battle is fierce. The enemy is relentless.

General Stormheart: (determined) We must hold the line. Every second counts. Fight with everything we have.

President Blackwell: (to the world leaders) This is our moment of truth. Our unity is our strength. Pray for our victory.

Priest: (leading a fervent prayer) Almighty God, protect us in this dark hour. Give strength to those who defend us. We place our trust in Your divine plan.

Congregation: Amen.

Asmodeus: (realizing the tides are turning) This cannot be! The key should have guaranteed our triumph!

Michael: (with divine authority) Your pride has blinded you, Asmodeus. The Lord's wisdom surpasses all. Your defeat was foretold.

As the battle rages, a brilliant light emanates from Michael, illuminating the battlefield. The forces of Hell begin to falter, their arrogance and pride turning to confusion and fear.

Asmodeus: (desperately) No! This cannot be!

Michael: (victorious) It is done. The Lord's justice prevails.

As the light fades, the celestial forces retreat, their pride shattered. Sanctaria stands strong, a testament to human resilience and divine intervention. The world breathes a collective sigh of relief, united in faith and hope.

General Stormheart: (to his troops) We did it. The battle is won, but we must remain vigilant. This victory is just the beginning.

President Blackwell: (addressing the world) We have faced the darkness and emerged victorious. Let this day be a reminder of our strength and unity. Together, we stand under God's protection.

Ena Katsumi calls on the Lord of hosts to re-force her angel comrades. Two portals to Heaven open in the sky above her mighty form. Thousands of mighty warrior angels pour through a portal of heavenly light, all trained for battle before the conflict by Michael and his angels. Weapons in hand, clad in heaven's best armor, ready to put a stop to the relentless evil. Micheal and his team swiftly soar in to intercept the bomb and see Ena and legions of angels surrounding her. Micheal: "Well, Ena, You're just a recruit, and you've made a huge difference. I'm here to Promote you to Arch- Angel". Ena was shocked. " I just did what God sent me to do and let him lead my steps."

Johphiel: You go sister that was amazing!

Costello: I've never known your seraphim were so cool.

Haniel: That epic transformation will go down in history as your defining moment. Glad to have you as part of the team!

Gabriel: Wow, no words

Uriel: who is powerful like our God

Raphael: I'm glad you're on our side, Ena.

Esther: That's how it's done. I see you've been studying our training. God bless you, Katsumi.

Sophia: I thought we were the coolest angels, but that was so powerful.

Ena: Thank you all. All Glory to the Lord of Hosts and Jesus Christ and The Holy Spirit, the source of my Power.

Micheal: It's nice to have a little reunion, but we have a people to save.

Asmodeus and the demon lords summon a dark portal. Every demon emerges, and Thousands of fallen angels descend onto the earth. Asmodeus and his fellow comrades Charge toward the angels. The clash of iron and steel rings throughout the earth as Evil and Good spare to death. Angels and demons were falling one by one. Eclipse and Sentinel force-locked in an inch-by-inch battle of epic proportions.

Satan, Satana, The Lawless One, Lilith, Jezebel, Bak'tor, Belial, Beelzebub, Behemoth, Judas, Death, Eisteth, and Asmodeus charge leading their servants into battle. The coven arms up to attack every church, but little do they know the Saints are ready to defend themselves. They don't want to kill, but self-defense is sanctioned in the bible. Enough is enough. Bullets wizz around as the Church engages the Conven hundreds fall in the battle. Baal, chained, sends his minions to Earth. Rock demons descend, getting into the fray. All Hell is literally breaking loose, and the fate of this realm will be decided in this battle.

The battle raged on, Michael and his angels fighting valiantly against the relentless demonic forces. The skies were darkened with the smoke of combat; the earth trembled under the weight of clashing powers. Though many demons lay wounded, they pressed on, driven by a malevolent determination.

Amidst the chaos, a strange sound filled the air, a low hum that grew into a deafening roar. The clouds parted to reveal a fleet of alien ships descending from the heavens. These extraterrestrial allies, known for their advanced technology and strategic prowess, had come to the aid of their demonic counterparts.

Michael, sensing a shift in the battle, rallied his angels for one final push. With a surge of divine energy, they redoubled their efforts, cutting through the demonic ranks with renewed ferocity. But the aliens, equipped with formidable weaponry, provided cover for the retreating demons, their ships acting as shields against the angelic onslaught.

SERAPHIM ANGEL ENA KATSUMI

The demons, battered but not broken, began to retreat towards the ships. One by one, they boarded, seeking refuge from the heavenly assault. The aliens, executing their escape plan with precision, lifted off from the war-torn landscape, taking the demons with them. The ships soared through the atmosphere, leaving the battlefield behind.

As the last ship disappeared into the sky, Michael stood tall, his sword glowing with celestial light. The earth was scarred, but it was not broken. He turned to his angels, their faces weary but resolute.

"The battle is won, but the war is not over," Michael declared. "We must remain vigilant. The forces of darkness will not rest, and neither shall we."

High above, the alien fleet sped through space, carrying their demonic passengers to a distant planet. There, they would regroup, and their defeat would be a temporary setback. They would plan, they would recover, and they would return. But for now, Earth was safe, protected by the unyielding strength of Michael and his angels.

In the silence that followed the battle, a sense of peace settled over the land. The angels, guardians of humanity, watched over the world with unwavering vigilance, ready to face whatever came next. And as the stars shone brightly in the night sky, the hope of a new dawn began to rise.

Ena sat at a small table in the bustling food court, savoring her meal. The mall was alive with the sounds of laughter, conversation, and the clinking of dishes. She enjoyed the anonymity of her human form, a brief respite from her true nature.

Suddenly, a deafening roar shattered the air, followed by a blinding flash of light. The ground shook violently, and within moments, the mall was consumed by a massive explosion. The force of the blast hurled Ena from her seat, sending her crashing to the ground, surrounded by debris and chaos.

Dazed and disoriented, she struggled to her feet, her ears ringing and her vision blurred. Through the dust and smoke, she saw panicked shoppers fleeing in every direction, their faces etched with terror. Ena's heart pounded as she tried to make sense of the destruction around her.

Above the cacophony, a new sound emerged—a deep, resonant hum that seemed to vibrate through her very bones. Ena looked up, and her eyes widened in disbelief. A colossal flying saucer hovered above the ruined mall, its sleek, metallic surface reflecting the fires below. The craft emitted a powerful pertrasonic boom, a sound so intense it felt like it could tear the fabric of reality itself.

Ena's instincts kicked in. She had to get out of there, had to find safety and understand what was happening. She began to navigate through the wreckage, helping those she could along the way. The mall, once a place of everyday normalcy, was now a war zone.

As she moved, fragments of memories surfaced—stories of ancient conflicts, of cosmic battles between celestial beings and otherworldly entities. The flying saucer above seemed to be a harbinger of such a conflict, and Ena felt an ominous connection to the unfolding events.

She found a small group of survivors huddled behind an overturned kiosk. "Are you okay?" she asked, her voice steady despite the chaos.

"Wh-what was that?" one of them stammered, eyes wide with fear.

"I'm not sure," Ena replied, "but we need to stay together and find a way out."

Just then, the saucer emitted another powerful pulse, sending shockwaves through the air. Ena's human form flickered, her true nature straining against the disguise. She took a deep breath, forcing herself to remain composed. There would be time to reveal herself if necessary, but for now, her priority was to protect these people.

As they made their way through the rubble, Ena couldn't shake the feeling that this was only the beginning. The explosion, the saucer—it all pointed to a larger threat, one that would require all her strength and cunning to confront.

For now, she had to survive and ensure these innocents did, too. But she knew that soon, very soon, she would have to face whatever force had brought such devastation and perhaps reveal her true form to stand against it?